# A Stand for Independence

## Independence

*A Felicity Classic*
*Volume 2*

*by* Valerie Tripp

Published by American Girl Publishing

Printed in China
17 18 19 20 21 22 23 LEO 8 7 6 5 4 3 2 1

This book is a work of fiction. Any similarity to real persons, living or dead,
is coincidental and not intended by American Girl. References to real events,
people, or places are used fictitiously. Other names, characters, places, and
incidents are the products of imagination.

Cover image by David Roth and Juliana Kolesova

Cataloging-in-Publication Data available from the Library of Congress

americangirl.com/service

*To Ann, Bobby, Katie, and Sarah*

*To the staffs of American Girl
and Colonial Williamsburg,
with thanks*

*To my husband, Michael,
and my daughter, Katherine,
with love*

# Beforever™

The adventurous characters you'll meet in
the BeForever books will spark your curiosity
about the past, inspire you to find your voice
in the present, and excite you about your future.
You'll make friends with these girls as you share
their fun and their challenges. Like you, they are
bright and brave, imaginative and energetic,
creative and kind. Just as you are, they are
discovering what really matters: Helping others.
Being a true friend. Protecting the earth.
Standing up for what's right. Read their stories,
explore their worlds, join their adventures.
Your friendship with them will BeForever.

# TABLE *of* CONTENTS

1   Springtime Promises ............................................. 1

2   Posie ..................................................................... 10

3   Grandmother's Guitar ......................................... 19

4   Drumbeats ........................................................... 28

5   The Long, Dark Night ....................................... 40

6   King's Creek Plantation ..................................... 51

7   Faithful Friends .................................................. 60

8   The Note in the Bird Bottle .............................. 71

9   Runaway ............................................................... 80

10   Penny Saves the Day ........................................... 90

11   A Cardinal and a Bluebird ............................... 100

12   Friends Divided ................................................ 108

13   Grandfather's Errand ....................................... 119

14   Into the Valley .................................................. 130

15   Patriot ................................................................ 141

Inside Felicity's World ............................................... 152

# Springtime Promises

elicity opened the kitchen window as wide as it would go and leaned toward the sunshine. The wind still had a whisper of winter in it. But the sun shone strong with the promise of spring-time, and the sky was a clean, clear blue.

It was spring cleaning day at the Merrimans'. Felicity was in the kitchen scrubbing the big silver chocolate pot in a tub of sudsy water. Her sister, Nan, and her brother, William, were helping her. That is, William was *supposed* to be helping. He was supposed to wash the wooden stirrer that went with the chocolate pot. Instead, William was using the stirrer as if it were a drumstick. He was happily hitting the water to make it splash up out of the tub.

Outside the kitchen window, Felicity could see Mother and Rose, the Merrimans' house servant, airing mattresses from all the beds in the household. They leaned the mattresses against the kitchen garden fence to freshen them in the bright spring sunshine.

Felicity spoke to her mother through the open window. "Mother," she said, "since Grandfather will be here with us on my birthday this year, do you think we might have a little party?"

Mrs. Merriman smiled at Felicity. "What sort of party?" she asked.

"Well," said Felicity as she thought, "it would be a small party. Just our family and Ben. It would be a celebration—a celebration of all of us being together and of spring." Felicity talked faster as her ideas poured out. "We could decorate the parlor with flowers. Grandfather loves flowers. I am sure tulips and daffodils will be blooming in my garden by then. We could use my favorite plates and our best chocolate cups. Oh! And we could have a fancy cake on the glass pyramid and—"

"Tarts!" interrupted Nan.

"Tarts and tarts and tarts!" added William.

"Yes, indeed," agreed Felicity. "Peach, blackberry, and raspberry tarts."

Mother laughed. "Lissie," she said, "you are always ahead of yourself. Your thoughts run off and away like wild ponies! You know 'tis days till Grandfather comes and weeks till your birthday." She helped Rose lift and turn one of the mattresses. "It's hard to believe you will be ten this year, Lissie," she said, "though you do grow fast as a weed. Perhaps that's what comes of being born in the spring."

"I like having a birthday in the spring," said Felicity. "Everything is blossoming and growing. The whole world is starting life new."

"Aye," agreed Mrs. Merriman. "The springtime suits you. You were born sooner than I expected. You couldn't wait to be born and start life new, as you say." She laughed. "You have been impatient and in a hurry ever since! Grandfather will be amazed to see how tall you've grown."

"Me, too," William said stoutly. "I'm taller, too!"

"Oh, much taller!" said Felicity. "We have lots of changes to show Grandfather. He hasn't even met Ben yet!" Ben was the apprentice in Mr. Merriman's store.

A small frown crossed Mrs. Merriman's face. Felicity realized her mother was afraid Ben might speak out in front of Grandfather. Ben did not think the colonies should belong to the King of England anymore. But Grandfather was a strict Loyalist. He would not take kindly to anyone who criticized the king!

Felicity looked down at the silver chocolate pot. She gently rubbed it dry. "Do you think Grandfather will be angry that we don't drink tea anymore?" she asked her mother. To protest the tax the king had set on tea, Mr. Merriman had stopped selling tea in his store, and the Merrimans had stopped drinking tea at home. "Will Grandfather mind drinking hot chocolate instead?"

Mrs. Merriman shook off her troubled look. "No one would mind chocolate poured from such a shiny pot!" she said cheerfully. "Now take off your wet apron. 'Tis time for you to go to your lessons at Miss Manderly's. Don't forget to stop at the house and fetch your hat. This spring sun will burn your nose quite pink!"

"Yes, Mother," said Felicity. She unpinned her apron and handed it to her mother. Then she skipped up to the house to tidy herself for lessons.

Felicity's best friend, Elizabeth, was waiting for her

at the pasture behind the Wythes' stable. They often
met there before lessons to visit the Wythes' mare and
her new colt. Elizabeth was standing on the bottom
rail of the fence watching the horses across the pasture.
When she saw Felicity, Elizabeth smiled. "Oh, good.
Here you are, Lissie," she said. "Do whistle and make
the horses come to us."

Felicity whistled. The mare trotted toward her,
and the colt followed behind like a little, shy shadow.
Elizabeth and Felicity pulled up handful after handful
of sweet spring grass and fed it to the horses.

Felicity giggled, "The colt's tongue is so wet and
rough, it tickles my hands." She wiped her hands with
her handkerchief, but they were still rather sticky and
quite green from the grass.

"I do love to visit those horses," Felicity said later.
She and Elizabeth were giving their hands a quick wash
at the Wythes' well. "They make me think of my horse
Penny. I hope Penny has not forgotten me."

Elizabeth's big blue eyes were serious. "Penny has
not forgotten you," she said. "You saved her from that
mean Mr. Nye, who beat her. You were patient with
her. You taught her to trust you. Now you must trust

*her*. Trust that she still loves you. Trust that she will come back to you if she can. Someday she will. I am sure."

Felicity smiled at her friend. Elizabeth always spoke straight from her heart.

The girls hurried along to their lessons. When they came into Miss Manderly's sunny parlor, they saw that Elizabeth's older sister, Annabelle, was already there, looking very prim. Annabelle put on a pained expression when she saw them. She sniffed, then held her handkerchief to her nose. Felicity grinned. She supposed she and Elizabeth must smell a tad horsey after their visit to the pasture.

"Good day, young ladies," said Miss Manderly. "Please be seated at the table. I have set up your needlework frames. Work quietly while Annabelle has her music lesson."

"Yes, Miss Manderly," said Elizabeth and Felicity. They sat at their needlework frames, facing each other across the table.

Felicity had finally finished her sampler of stitches at the end of the winter. When Miss Manderly said she was ready to move on to more difficult stitchery,

Felicity was very pleased. She loved the wooden needlework frame that sat so prettily on the table in front of her. The frame held the linen taut while she made her stitches.

A gentle spring breeze played with the leaves outside the window. They seemed to dance with the soft music Miss Manderly was strumming on Annabelle's guitar. When Miss Manderly began to sing, it seemed to Felicity that the sound filled the room with color and light.

Then Miss Manderly handed the guitar to Annabelle. Oh no! Felicity and Elizabeth looked at each other and tried not to groan. For now it was Annabelle's turn to play and sing.

Horrible sounds filled the room and chased away all the beautiful music. When Annabelle played, the guitar sounded whiny, tinny, and twangy. And her singing was even worse.

*"In spite of all my friends could say, young Colin stole my heart away,"* warbled Annabelle.

"Indeed, I wish someone would steal *all* of her away," Elizabeth whispered. "She sings as if her stays are laced too tight."

Felicity laughed softly. But secretly, she was envious of Annabelle. She wished with all her heart she were old enough to learn to play the guitar. But she knew young ladies did not begin music lessons until they were twelve or thirteen years old.

Felicity looked at Annabelle's guitar out of the corners of her eyes. It was made of shiny wood, shaped like half a pear, with a long, slender neck. Felicity hated to admit it, but Annabelle looked grown-up and elegant when she held the guitar. Felicity longed to strum the guitar and to touch the luscious satin ribbon Annabelle had tied to it.

When at last Annabelle stopped singing and playing, Felicity went over to her. "Annabelle," she asked, "may I hold your guitar?"

"Oh, dear me, no!" said Annabelle. She held the guitar closer to her. "Papa just bought this guitar. It was very costly. You are far too, too . . . you simply may not touch it!"

Felicity flushed.

Miss Manderly said, "I am sure Felicity will be careful, Annabelle."

Felicity started to hold out her hands. Annabelle

pulled back as if she'd seen a snake. "Gracious me!" she exclaimed. "Look at your hands! They are *green*! They are filthy!"

Felicity glanced at her hands and then quickly hid them behind her back. They were only the tiniest bit grass-stained. They were *not* filthy. "I beg your pardon," Felicity said in a cold voice. She turned on her heel and stalked back to her chair. Snippy Annabelle! She could *keep* her precious guitar.

# Posie

## CHAPTER 2

**M**orning after morning, the spring days burst into beauty like blossoming flowers. Morning after morning, Felicity worked hard to prepare her garden for Grandfather's inspection. He was due to arrive any day now. Felicity wanted her garden to look perfect for him.

Grandfather had taught Felicity many things about gardening. He believed gardens should be orderly, well kept, and useful as well as beautiful. That is why Felicity had vegetables and herbs growing in tidy rows next to her flowers.

Felicity loved to feel the rich, dark earth so cool and heavy in her hands. It smelled of sun and rain. The little seedlings pushed up out of the earth, first as a soft green fuzz and then as slender, budding stems. Each flower was different. Each was determined to stand up and offer its face to the sun. But weeds wanted to grow, too. There was one weed in particular that was especially stubborn. No matter how many times Felicity dug out its tough green stem, the spiky weed came back.

"I think you had better let that weed grow," said Ben. He was leaning over the garden fence, grinning at Felicity. "You can't seem to discourage it."

Felicity grinned back at Ben. "I don't truly mind it," she said. "Indeed, I rather like it. 'Tis so stubborn. But I know Grandfather would not approve. And I want Grandfather to think my garden is in fine order."

"Well," said Ben. "Things that grow have a will of their own. 'Tis hard indeed to stop them." He stuck the stem of the weed in his buttonhole. Suddenly, Ben stood up straight. He called out, "Good day, Isaac!"

Isaac was a free black just a little older than Ben. He and his family did laundry work at their home on the edge of town. Several times a month, Isaac came to the Merrimans' house to pick up laundry to be washed or to return clean laundry.

Isaac came toward Felicity and Ben. He set down the laundry basket. "Good day to you," he said with a smile. "Felicity, your garden is fine indeed!"

"Thank you, Isaac," said Felicity.

"Isaac," said Ben earnestly. "You are a drummer with the militia, aren't you?"

"Aye," answered Isaac. "That I am."

"Will you teach me how to play beats on your drum?" asked Ben.

"Me, too?" asked Felicity.

"Very well," said Isaac. "I don't have my drum with me now. But I can give you both a quick lesson anyway." He picked up two sticks from the ground and held them as if they were drumsticks.

"The drums are very important to the militia," Isaac explained. "They tell the soldiers what to do. Different drumbeats mean different things. This beat tells everyone to wake up." Isaac beat a loud, insistent beat on the garden fence. *Rat tat TAT! Rat tat TAT!* "And this beat tells the men to come quickly and line up with their guns." Isaac played a louder beat. *Brrrrump pum pumpety! Brrrrump pum pumpety!* "And this beat is my favorite. It's called 'roast beef.' It means dinner is ready." Isaac beat a lively roll. *Pumpety pumpety pumpety pum!*

Isaac gave Ben the sticks, and Ben tried playing the

beats. Then Felicity had a turn. "You do well, Felicity," Isaac smiled.

Ben glanced at Felicity. Then he said to Isaac in a low voice, "I made a delivery to the Raleigh Tavern yesterday morning. I heard a rumor that Governor Dunmore has the key to the Magazine, where all the colonists' gunpowder is stored. They say the governor wants to have his marines take all the gunpowder away."

Felicity spoke up, "But if the governor's men took our gunpowder, that would be stealing. Why would the governor do such a thing?"

"The governor is afraid," Isaac said gravely. "He knows the colony's militia is practicing more often. He is afraid the colonists will use the gunpowder in the Magazine to fight against him and the British soldiers. He fears the time is coming when the colonists will fight for their independence."

"But the governor isn't a *thief*," insisted Felicity. "He wouldn't *steal*."

Isaac said softly, "A frightened man may do anything."

Ben sighed. "Lissie, things have changed a great

deal since you went dancing at the Governor's Palace in January," he said. "The king has sent more and more British troops here. It looks as if the British are getting ready to fight. Relations between Loyalists and Patriots have grown much worse. Many people are beginning to distrust the governor because he is the king's representative here."

Felicity shook her head. She said, "I am *sure* . . . "

"Nothing is sure, when trust is gone," said Ben.

Felicity hoped Ben wouldn't say anything in front of Grandfather about people distrusting the governor. Grandfather would be terribly displeased.

The very next afternoon, Felicity floated home from lessons humming the minuet Miss Manderly had played on Annabelle's guitar that day. She danced into the stable yard, then stopped. Marcus, Father's man-servant, was unharnessing a horse from a dusty riding chair. She knew that riding chair. It belonged to Grandfather!

"Grandfather!" Felicity shouted happily as she ran into the parlor. There he was, standing with Father, brushing the dust off his coat.

Grandfather made Felicity an elegant bow. "Good day," he said formally. "Do I have the honor of addressing Miss Felicity Merriman? The young lady who attended a dance lesson at the royal Governor's Palace?"

"Oh, Grandfather!" laughed Felicity as she hugged him. "I am so glad you are here. I must tell you all about the dance at the Palace. 'Twas very fine! And there's a new colt at the Wythes', and you must see my garden, and . . . "

"Did you plant the herbs and vegetables near the kitchen as I told you, and the sweet-smelling flowers nearest the house?" Grandfather asked.

"Aye!" said Felicity. "Everything is growing nicely, but there is one weed that is so stubborn it will not go away."

"Stubborn, you say?" said Grandfather. "Let's go have a look at it. Perhaps I know its name and how to tame it."

"Now, Father," said Mrs. Merriman as she carried in a pitcher of cool water to drink. "You just arrived. Are you not hot and tired?"

"Aye!" said Grandfather with a smile. "So the garden is the very place for me. No place is more refreshing than a garden, eh, Felicity?"

Felicity nodded happily and took his hand.

"And," said Grandfather, "there's someone outside Felicity must meet."

"Oh, very well," laughed Mrs. Merriman. "Go along with you!" She and Mr. Merriman smiled as Felicity and Grandfather hurried out into the sunshine.

Grandfather was a tall, spare gentleman who stood very straight. He wore no wig, but instead tied his white hair back in a queue. His soft gray eyes were usually full of gentle good humor.

Felicity skipped next to Grandfather, wondering whom she was to meet. Just as they reached the garden gate, William ran up to her and pulled her by the hand. "Come, Lissie! See what Grandfather has brought us!" he cried. "Look!"

In a far corner of the garden, Felicity saw Nan holding what looked like a lapful of soft white fluff. Suddenly, the fluff bleated! Felicity hurried toward Nan. She knelt and looked into the small, sweet face of a lamb.

"Ohhhh," sighed Felicity. "Ohhhh! What a dear! Oh,

Grandfather! I've never seen such a love!" The lamb looked at Felicity with big, gentle eyes. Felicity patted the lamb's soft fleece. "Is the lamb ours?" Felicity asked. "May we care for her?"

"Well," said Grandfather slowly. "I believe it is a good thing for children to have animals to care for. It reminds them that they are not the only living creatures on the earth. But taking care of an animal is a big responsibility. Do you think I can trust you to raise this lamb properly?"

"Oh, yes!" said Nan, William, and Felicity all at once.

Grandfather smiled. "Very well then," he said. "If you do a good job, the lamb may stay here. But if I see that you are irresponsible, I shall take the lamb back to my farm. Is that fair?"

"Yes!" said Nan and William.

"Thank you, Grandfather," said Felicity. Nan put the lamb in Felicity's lap. Then she and William ran off to tell Mother and Father about Grandfather's gift.

Grandfather sat down on the bench next to Felicity. "I know this little lamb won't replace your Penny," he said. "But perhaps she can be a comfort to you."

Felicity smiled at Grandfather. She hugged the lamb gently. "Thank you, Grandfather," she said again. "Thank you."

Nan and William came back, dragging Mother and Father with them.

"See the lamb, Mother?" said Nan. "See how little she is?"

"What will you call your new pet?" asked Mother.

Felicity laughed as the lamb stood on its shaky legs and wobbled right into the middle of some flowers. "I think we should call the lamb Posie," Felicity said, "because that will remind us of where she will be if we don't keep an eye on her!"

# Grandmother's Guitar

## CHAPTER 3

**S**pring kept its promise of beautiful days. Huge white clouds sailed across the gloriously blue sky. The apple trees were heavy with pink blossoms, and the air was sweet with their delicious scent.

Felicity loved being with Grandfather. Elizabeth did, too. She joined them in the garden almost every day before lessons. Grandfather sat in the shade with Posie at his feet. He watched Felicity weed, water, and prune her plants. Elizabeth made miniature landscapes out of the cuttings. She used twigs and stems for trees and moss for grass. Buds and petals were her flowers, and leaves were her ferns.

One afternoon, Grandfather studied Elizabeth's landscape. "What place have you made here?" he asked. "This is a miniature of a real garden, is it not?"

"Oh, 'tis my garden at home—I mean, in England," answered Elizabeth.

Grandfather nodded. "You miss it, do you?" he asked.

"Aye," said Elizabeth. "My family came here to Virginia in the fall. This is my first spring away from England."

Felicity sat back on her heels and looked at Elizabeth. She had never heard Elizabeth speak this way before. She had never thought about Elizabeth missing England.

Grandfather spoke thoughtfully. "I grew up in England, too," he said to Elizabeth. "I, too, was transplanted to the soil of another country. 'Tis not easy to feel at home in a new place."

Elizabeth sighed. "You see, sir, my parents are Loyalists," she said. "And some people here have different ideas. They say the colonies should not belong to the king anymore. 'Tis hard to know what to think."

"Humph!" snorted Grandfather. "All this talk against the king and his governor is stuff and nonsense! 'Tis the ranting of irresponsible scoundrels. The colonies are part of England and will be so forevermore."

Felicity looked at Grandfather's stern face. *It's a good thing he did not hear Ben and Isaac talking about the governor,* she thought. She went back to her digging.

Felicity did not want to hear any more disturbing talk about the king and England. But it seemed to follow her like an unwelcome, bothersome fly. That evening, after supper, Ben went off to visit a friend. After Ben left, Grandfather frowned.

"You had better keep an eye on that young man," Grandfather said to Father. "He is much too interested in the militia. He'll be shirking his duties at the store to sneak off and watch them muster if you don't stop him."

"Ben is a good lad," said Father. "I trust him."

"Humph!" said Grandfather. "How can you trust someone you know is disloyal to the king? I heard Ben say the colonies should be independent. These young Patriots talking about rebellion know nothing about trust or loyalty. They have forgotten that loyalty is a promise to honor our old and valuable traditions."

"Aye, sir," said Father. "We must honor traditions. But perhaps we must honor new ideas, too."

"Balderdash!" sputtered Grandfather. "New ideas

are new nonsense! People are nothing if they are not loyal to their old values and traditions. They are irresponsible—"

"Now, now," interrupted Mrs. Merriman. "Please let us have no arguing and disharmony. I hope there is room in the world for old ideas *and* new ideas, just as there is room for, for . . . " She looked around the room and smiled when she saw the spinet. "Just as there is room for old songs and new songs." She sat at the spinet and started to play. "Let us sing together."

Felicity could see that Grandfather was still cross. But he and Father were gentlemen, so they politely joined in the singing. And soon enough, the music soothed and cheered everyone.

"Felicity, my dear," said Grandfather. "You have a fine voice. I think perhaps you have your grandmother's gift for music. I have brought something for you. Wait here."

He left the room for a short while. When he came back, Felicity could hardly believe her eyes. Grandfather handed her a guitar! A beautiful, graceful guitar! It was made of the same shiny wood as Annabelle's guitar, but Felicity thought it was much finer. It had a flower carved in the middle where Annabelle's guitar had only a hole.

Felicity hardly dared to touch the guitar. She looked up at Grandfather and asked, "Is this . . . is this for *me?*"

"Aye," said Grandfather. "It belonged to your dear grandmother. You must promise to be very careful with it." He glanced at Father and said firmly, "It is old and valuable, and so it is something to be treasured."

"Indeed, yes," said Mrs. Merriman quickly. "We shall keep the guitar in the house, in the parlor, where it will be safe."

Felicity cradled the guitar in her arms. She felt as if she had been given something magic, something full of enchanting music waiting to come out, waiting for *her* to bring it out. She brushed the strings with her fingertips. They were out of tune, and the fine old ribbon tied to the guitar was frayed. But to Felicity the guitar was perfection. It *was* a treasure.

"Thank you, Grandfather," she said. "I promise to take good care of the guitar. Someday, when I am older, I'll play it for you. We'll sing together."

Grandfather's eyes were their softest gray. "Indeed we shall, my dear girl," he said. "I know you will guard it well and keep it from harm. You are a young lady to be trusted."

Later that night, when she was lying in bed, an idea wormed its way into Felicity's thoughts. *Now I have a guitar*, she realized. *I have a guitar that is finer than Annabelle's. How I wish I could show it to her!* Felicity quickly reminded herself that Mother had said the guitar must be kept in the parlor so that it would be safe. She was not to take the guitar out of the house. So Felicity tried to push the idea away. But somehow, it would not go.

Days passed, and soon it was April twentieth, the day before Felicity's birthday. That afternoon, Mother, Nan, William, and Grandfather went to visit old Mr. Fitchett. They left before Felicity went to lessons, and they were not due back until early evening.

After Felicity waved good-bye to them, she wandered into the parlor and took the guitar down from the tall bookcase. She plucked the strings. *'Tis too bad the guitar is so out of tune,* she thought. She tried to tighten the strings herself, as she had seen Miss Manderly do when she was tuning Annabelle's guitar. But she did not know how the notes were supposed to sound. Felicity put the guitar back in its place. She stared up at it.

*Perhaps,* she thought, *perhaps Miss Manderly would tune the guitar for me. And perhaps Miss Manderly could teach me a song to play at our party tomorrow! That would be a fine surprise for everyone. Surely Mother and Grandfather would not mind if I took the guitar out of the house for such a good purpose. Indeed, I should think they would be pleased.*

But in her heart, Felicity knew Mother and Grandfather would not be pleased if she took the guitar without asking. And in her heart she knew the real reason she wanted to bring the guitar to Miss Manderly's house. She wanted Annabelle to see it. She wanted to make Annabelle jealous.

Quickly, before she could think more carefully, Felicity took the guitar down from the bookcase again. Her hands were cold as she carried it out the door and along the street. She had a sickly feeling in the bottom of her stomach that she was doing something wrong, but she walked briskly to her lessons, as if she could leave the feeling behind her.

Elizabeth gasped when Felicity entered Miss Manderly's parlor. "Oh, Lissie!" Elizabeth exclaimed. "You brought your grandmother's guitar, the guitar you told me about. It *is* beautiful!"

Felicity knew Annabelle was staring at the guitar as she handed it to Miss Manderly. "My grandfather gave me this guitar," Felicity said proudly. "I was wondering if you might tune it for me?"

Miss Manderly smiled. "I should be pleased to," she said. "This is a fine old instrument, Felicity." She tuned the strings and then strummed a few chords. "Hear the depth of sound it has. Such a rich tone!" She handed the guitar back to Felicity. "Guard this well," she said. "It is a work of art."

"Felicity," said Annabelle in a sweet voice. "I did not bring my guitar today. May I hold yours? I will show you how to play a tune."

"Thank you, Annabelle," Felicity said politely. "But I think Miss Manderly and I must be the only ones to hold the guitar. 'Tis very old and very precious. I promised to be most careful with it."

"Indeed!" said Annabelle. She looked at the guitar again with a little pout on her face. Then she looked away.

Felicity turned to Miss Manderly. "Would you teach me to play a little, Miss Manderly?" she asked.

"Just a chord or two, or a short tune?"

Felicity held the guitar, and Miss Manderly placed her fingers on the strings. It was more difficult to make music than Felicity had thought, but she tried very hard. And the old guitar seemed eager to sound beautiful.

"You have a good ear and a firm touch, Felicity," said Miss Manderly. "When you are old enough for serious lessons, you will do well."

Annabelle pretended not to hear, but Felicity knew she was listening because her pout grew poutier. When lessons were over, Annabelle flounced out ahead of Elizabeth and Felicity. Felicity smiled to herself. *Annabelle is envious of my guitar!* she thought. Felicity was pleased. She had forgotten about the sickly feeling in her stomach.

# Drumbeats

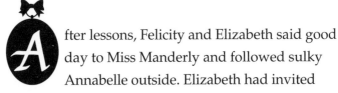fter lessons, Felicity and Elizabeth said good day to Miss Manderly and followed sulky Annabelle outside. Elizabeth had invited Felicity to spend the afternoon at her house. Mrs. Cole, Elizabeth and Annabelle's mother, greeted them at the door in a flutter of confusion.

"Girls, girls, girls," she said. "Do be quiet! Your father has some very important visitors. British military men! Officers!"

"Officers?" said Annabelle, perking up. "Shall I play and sing for them?" She patted her hair and fluffed her petticoats.

"Oh, dear me, no!" exclaimed Mrs. Cole. "No, you must be quiet as mice. Go to your rooms. Or better yet, go out to the garden, won't you?"

"Humph!" exclaimed Annabelle. She swept up the

28

stairs to her bedchamber in a huff.

Felicity and Elizabeth happily went outside and sat on a bench under the leafy arbor. Felicity played the tune Miss Manderly had taught her. The guitar sounded even lovelier outside in the spring air. Elizabeth hummed along. After a while, she wandered about the garden, picking flowers. Felicity played on and on. What a pleasure it was to play the guitar!

"Lissie," Elizabeth called. "Do come here and tell me the names of these flowers. They are such a pretty pink."

Felicity leaned the guitar against the bench. She skipped over to join Elizabeth and look at the flowers. "Those flowers are called sweet William," Felicity said. "But somehow they do not quite remind me of my brother William. They are so pink and proper, and he is usually so muddy!"

Elizabeth laughed. "Let's pick some," she said, kneeling down. "We can use the blossoms to make a flower necklace for Posie and pompons to put in *our* hair."

"Oh, that is a fine idea," agreed Felicity, joining her. The two girls picked small handfuls of sweet William.

Then Felicity asked, "Do you have any violets? They would look lovely in your fair hair."

"I think there are violets growing in front of the house," said Elizabeth.

"Let's go look," said Felicity. She and Elizabeth walked around to the gardens in front of the house. Suddenly, Felicity heard the low rumble of drums. "Listen!" she said. "Do you hear the drums? The militia must be mustering on the green."

"What does *mustering* mean?" asked Elizabeth.

"Mustering is when the men in the militia get together to practice marching and shooting and following orders," explained Felicity. "Come! Let's go watch."

"I don't think I want to," said Elizabeth. "Let's go see Posie."

"We'll see Posie *after* the muster," said Felicity impatiently. She grabbed Elizabeth's hand and pulled her out the front gate, along the street, and across Market Square to the green next to the Magazine. A large crowd had gathered to watch the men muster.

Felicity and Elizabeth wove their way through the crowd until they found Ben. Ben grinned when he saw Felicity. "I knew you'd come when you heard the drums," he said. He pointed to the drummers. "Look. There's Isaac."

Felicity saw Isaac with his drum. Just then the fife players began to pipe a sharp, lively tune. Isaac and the other drummers beat upon their drums. The men shouldered their guns and marched in rows behind the drummers. Little boys ran alongside, shouting with excitement. The men marched smartly across the green, in step with the drumbeats, their guns glinting in the sun. Felicity felt the drumbeats thunk in her stomach. The fife music gave her goose bumps on her arms. And when the men stopped, turned, and fired their guns into the air, Felicity's heart jumped.

"Oh!" exclaimed Elizabeth beside her. "Let's go *home*!"

Felicity turned to her in surprise. "But it's so exciting!" she said.

Elizabeth looked miserable. "I think it's scary," she said. "I'm going. Good-bye." She ran off before Felicity could say another word.

Felicity soon forgot everything as she stood next to Ben, watching and listening. She tried to name the drumbeats Isaac and the other drummers were playing.

She counted the rows of men and studied the horses the officers rode. She sniffed the air. It was heavy with smoke and dust and the burnt tang of gunpowder.

Felicity felt proud of the militia men. "They look fine, don't they, Ben?" she said. "I know the men in the colonists' militia are just citizens and not paid soldiers like the king's soldiers. But they do look fine today."

Ben was so intent watching the muster that Felicity thought he did not hear her. His arms were folded across his chest, and his eyes were wide.

Then he nodded. "The militia has been practicing more often since March," he said. "Militias in every county in Virginia have been practicing more. We have to be ready to defend ourselves."

"In a fight against the king's soldiers?" asked Felicity.

"Aye," said Ben.

Suddenly, it struck Felicity. She realized why Elizabeth was frightened. These men were not practicing just to make excitement. They were practicing to get ready to fight and to die if they had to. And whom would they have to fight? They would fight soldiers, real soldiers, British soldiers, the best soldiers in the world. These men might die because they did not want to be ruled by the King of England anymore. They were ready to give their lives to be independent. Then the argument against the king would no longer be about drinking tea or not drinking tea. It would be a matter of life and death. Felicity shivered. This time it was not a shiver of excitement. It was dread.

Clouds covered the sun. As the muster was dismissed, a soft rain began to fall like a chilly veil. Felicity and Ben walked home quietly.

"I wish more than anything I could join the militia like Isaac," said Ben. "I'd give anything to be able to fight." His voice was full of longing.

Felicity looked over at him. "But you cannot join the militia, Ben," she said. "You are an apprentice. Apprentices are not allowed to join. 'Tis in your agreement with Father. Is it not?"

"Aye," said Ben in a low voice. "I cannot join the militia as long as I am an apprentice. But . . . "

"Ben!" Felicity said sharply. "You wouldn't break your agreement with Father! He trusts you! You'd never run away, would you? You *couldn't*."

Ben looked at her and said nothing.

Felicity burst out. "You are our friend, Ben! You are part of our family. It wouldn't be honorable to run away."

Ben gave Felicity a sad grin. "I won't do anything while your grandfather is here," he said. "Your grandfather would be furious."

"Aye," said Felicity. "Grandfather has strict ideas. He . . . " Suddenly Felicity stopped stock still. "Oh no! Oh *no*!" she cried. "Grandfather! The guitar! Oh, Ben! I forgot! I *forgot*! I left the guitar at Elizabeth's house!" Felicity grabbed Ben's arm with both hands and spoke quickly. "I must run to the Coles' and get the guitar. If Mother and Grandfather are home, tell them I am on my way! But don't tell them about the guitar! They will be angry."

"Aye!" said Ben. "Run! Run fast!"

Felicity took off as fast as her feet could go. Her heart pounded as she ran through the gray drizzle. If only she could sneak the guitar back home before Mother and Grandfather returned. Oh, how she wished she had not been so thoughtless!

Felicity was a fast runner. In a few minutes, she reached the Coles' house. She ran back to the garden

and hurried toward the arbor where she had left
the guitar. Ah! She panted with relief. There it was,
propped against the bench just where she had left it.
But when Felicity reached for the guitar, she saw
someone coming. It was Mr. Cole and a British officer.
Felicity did not want them to see her, so she ducked
behind a bush. She hugged the guitar to her chest.

The British officer was speaking in a serious voice.
"The governor's marines are about five miles away,
at Burwell's Landing on the James River," said the
officer. "They'll come very late tonight and take the
gunpowder out of the Magazine."

Felicity froze. She could not believe her ears.

The officer went on, "Governor Dunmore will tell
the people of Williamsburg that he heard rumor of a
slave uprising. He'll say the gunpowder was removed
for the colonists' own protection."

Mr. Cole spoke up. "The people will know that's a
lie and that the governor has stolen their gunpowder,"
he said. "Everyone knows the governor is afraid the colonists will use the gunpowder to fight against him and
our British soldiers. 'Tis sad indeed when the governor
must stoop to such low deeds as lying and stealing."

The officer sounded angry. "I beg your pardon, sir!" he said.

"Aye," said Mr. Cole. "We must all beg pardon for what the governor is about to do. This will destroy any last shred of trust the colonists have in him. I am loyal to the king, but I am sorry to be involved in such deeds." He sighed. "Very well, then," he said to the officer. "You may go. I have received your report."

The two men walked away, but Felicity did not move. The British officer's words echoed in her head. *The marines are going to take the gunpowder tonight!* She had to tell someone! They must be stopped! What on earth was she going to do? What could she possibly do?

Felicity ran home holding the guitar close to her. She was full of fear and confusion.

When Felicity stepped into the house, her heart sank. Mother, Father, and Grandfather all sat in the parlor. Felicity put the guitar behind her back.

Mrs. Merriman looked up with a smile. "There you are, Lissie," she said. "Were you playing with Posie? We shall . . . " She stopped. The smile faded from her face. "Felicity, what is the matter? You look a fright! And what do you have behind your back?" Mrs.

Merriman came over to Felicity. "Why, it's the guitar," she said as she took it away. "And just look at it! The ribbon is torn through! The guitar is wet! Felicity! What *have* you done?"

Felicity could not meet her mother's eyes. "I'm sorry. Truly I am. I meant no harm," she said. "I just wanted Miss Manderly to tune it and . . . and I wanted Annabelle to see it."

"You took the guitar?" asked Mother. "But you were most clearly told not to take it out of this house. And how did it get so wet?"

"Well, I . . . it was a mistake," said Felicity. "I was playing it at Elizabeth's house, and then we went to the muster, and I . . . I forgot it."

Felicity hung her head. She had never felt so ashamed in her life.

Mrs. Merriman looked angry and sad at the same time. She handed the guitar back to Felicity. "Show your grandfather what you have done. You must ask him to forgive you," she said.

Felicity slowly carried the guitar to Grandfather. Her eyes filled with tears. "I'm sorry, Grandfather," she whispered. "Please forgive me. I am so sorry."

Grandfather took the guitar and touched the bedraggled ribbon. He frowned. "I was wrong to bring the guitar here," he said. "I see now that you are too young to be trusted with something so valuable."

"Go to bed, Felicity," said Father. "Think about what you have done."

Felicity started to go. She wanted to run from the room, run from the house, and never face any of them ever again. But she made herself stop and turn around. "Father," she said. "Please listen to me."

Mr. Merriman nodded. "What is it?" he asked.

Felicity took a deep breath. "When I went back to the Coles' house to fetch the guitar just now, I heard Mr. Cole talking to a British officer. The officer said that . . . " Mother, Father, and Grandfather were frowning at her, but Felicity forced herself to go on. "The officer said that British marines would come tonight to take the gunpowder out of the Magazine. And Mr. Cole said it was stealing, but—"

"Stop!" growled Grandfather. His eyes were dark as thunderclouds. "Stop this wild talk! 'Tis foolish, irresponsible, shameful! Stop it, I say!" He shook his head in anger. "Felicity, I am sorely disappointed in you!"

Felicity was rigid with shame.

Father sighed. "Felicity, how can you expect us to believe such a tale?" he asked. "You have shown yourself to be dishonest and irresponsible in the matter of the guitar. How can we possibly trust you?"

"But Father," Felicity said, "I did hear them! I did!"

Father held up his hand. "Don't disgrace yourself further by spreading wild falsehoods, especially about such serious matters," he said sternly. "Go now. We have heard enough from you for one evening."

# The Long, Dark Night

### ❧ CHAPTER 5 ❧

F elicity gave up. She trudged up the stairs to her bedchamber. She had never felt so miserable in her life. She threw herself on her bed and wept bitterly.

Felicity cried until she had no more tears. Then she sat by her window, watching the rain fall softly, silently, until the sky was dark. She wished with all her heart she had not taken the guitar. She wished she had not left the guitar at Elizabeth's house. Most of all, she wished she had not heard Mr. Cole and the officer talking. The burden of what she had heard them say was too heavy for her to bear. She wanted to forget it. But she could not. She knew she had to tell someone about the plan to steal the gunpowder. There were only two people who could help her—Ben and Isaac.

Felicity waited until she could no longer hear the

deep murmur of voices from the parlor. When the
house was quiet, and everyone else was asleep, she
tiptoed out of her room.

Down the stairs she went without making a sound.
She hurried out the door, across the yard, and to Ben's
room above the stable. When Felicity got to Ben's door,
she found it was closed tight and latched. How could
she wake him? If she called to him, she'd wake Marcus
and the horses.

Felicity had an idea. With her finger, she tapped
the drumbeat Isaac had taught her. *Rat tat TAT! Rat tat
TAT! Rat tat TAT!* Once, twice, three times she tapped
the beat that meant *wake up!*

It worked. Ben opened the door. "Lissie!" he
gasped. "What is it? What—"

"Shhh!" cautioned Felicity. "Listen! It's *tonight,* Ben.
The marines are coming to steal the gunpowder tonight.
I heard an officer say so when I was at the Coles'. Come
quick! We've got to wake Isaac. We need his drum."

Ben looked dazed. "Lissie . . . " he began.

"Come *now!*" hissed Felicity impatiently. "We have
no time to waste!"

Ben nodded. He pulled on his coat and followed

Felicity out of the stable. Quiet as cats, they ran through the eerie darkness.

At the street corner, Felicity stopped. "You go to the Magazine," she said to Ben. "The marines may be there already. Shout as loud as you can if you see anything. I'll go get Isaac."

"Aye," said Ben. He disappeared.

Felicity hurried on. The sky was so clouded, she felt as if she were swimming through black water without a single star to guide her. Alone, she ran through the deserted town, past the back streets, to Isaac's house. Felicity knew Isaac and his brother slept in a shed attached to the back of the house. She crept up to the door and rattled it.

"Isaac!" she whispered. "Isaac! Wake up!"

Isaac opened the door a crack. "Felicity!" he said. "What's the matter?"

"Come with me. You've got to," said Felicity. "The marines are going to steal the gunpowder *tonight*. Ben is already at the Magazine, keeping watch. You must come and bring your drum to sound the alarm."

Isaac looked hard at Felicity. "It is very dangerous for a black person like me to be seen on the streets in town at night," he said. "If I were found . . . " He shook his head. "It would not go well for me."

"I know," said Felicity. "But you must trust me, Isaac. We've got to stop them from stealing the powder. Please. You must help."

Isaac didn't say another word. He picked up his drum and drumsticks, grabbed a cloak, and followed Felicity.

They found Ben crouched against the brick wall that surrounded the Magazine. "Nothing yet," he whispered. "And look. There's no guard here tonight. Someone is definitely up to no good."

Isaac, Ben, and Felicity huddled together in the rainy darkness. Isaac covered himself and his drum with his cloak. Hour after hour, they waited. The night became colder, wetter, and blacker. They heard nothing. They saw nothing.

"It is well past midnight," whispered Isaac.

Felicity was too cold and too frightened to be tired. Doubt began to creep into her mind, cold as the chill from the rain. Over and over, she repeated to herself what she had heard the officer say to Mr. Cole. *The governor's marines are about five miles away, at Burwell's*

*Landing on the James River. They'll come very late tonight and take the gunpowder out of the Magazine.* She had not misunderstood, had she? She *couldn't* be wrong.

Ben shifted restlessly and sighed. Isaac accidentally knocked his foot against his drum. *Clunk!* Then, a moment later: *Clunk!* Felicity tensed. She held her breath. *Clunk!* There it was again! That was the unmistakable sound of a cart. *Clink!* That was the sound of a harness. Then Felicity heard footsteps. Ben and Isaac looked at her. They heard the sounds, too.

"Lift me up so I can see," whispered Felicity.

She stood on their shoulders and peeked over the top of the wall surrounding the Magazine. By the light of a lantern, men were loading barrels of gunpowder onto a cart. They worked quickly and quietly, their shoulders hunched against the rain.

Felicity slipped to the ground. "The marines are in there! They are loading the gunpowder onto a cart!" she said. "Beat your drum, Isaac! Beat it as loud as you can!"

Isaac flung back his cloak. He pulled the drum strap over his shoulder and began to pound on his drum with all his might. *Brrrrump pum pumpety! Brrrrump pum pumpety!* The drumbeats crashed like thunder. The marines shouted in surprise. *Brrrump pum pumpety! Brrrrump pum pumpety!* The Magazine seemed to shake with the force of the drumbeats. Isaac's strong arms pounded and pounded his drum. *Brrrrump pum pumpety! Brrrrump pum pumpety!*

Felicity could hear the marines calling out to each other and clambering into the cart. The whip snapped, the horse whinnied wildly, and suddenly the cart rumbled out the gate of the Magazine and down the street, as fast as it could go.

*Brrrump pum pumpety! Brrrrump pum pumpety!* Still Isaac beat on. Ben and Felicity ran from house to house, beating on the doors, banging on the windows. They shouted as loud as they could, "Make haste! Come quick! The marines have stolen our gunpowder! Hurry!" And all the while, Isaac beat his drum. *Brrrrump pum pumpety! Brrrrump pum pumpety!*

Windows flew open. People poured out of their houses carrying burning torches. They ran to the Magazine, shouting to one another in wild confusion. In no time, a mob had gathered. Their faces were angry in the fiery torch light. Their loud voices filled the night with noise, drowning out the beat of Isaac's drum.

"They've stolen our gunpowder!" voice after voice cried. "It's gone!"

"The governor will answer for this!"

"This is thievery! Villainy! Our gunpowder is gone!"

"The governor's behind this! He must pay!"

Felicity could feel anger sweep through the crowd of people. Isaac caught her eye and nodded. Then he slipped away to go home. Felicity and Ben sank out of the circle of torch light. Felicity was suddenly weary. She was glad when she saw Father's face coming toward her through the blur of the crowd.

"Felicity!" said Father. "Ben! What on earth are you two doing here?"

"We sounded the alarm, sir," said Ben to Mr. Merriman. "We saw the marines stealing the gunpowder, and we sounded the alarm." His voice was proud.

Felicity lifted a tired face to her father. "I had to do it, Father," she said. "I know you will be angry. But I had to do it."

Mr. Merriman put his arm around Felicity's shoulders. "Come along now," he said. "Both of you. It is dangerous here. You belong at home."

## ๊ The Long, Dark Night ๊

Ben, Father, and Felicity walked home, leaving the fiery torches, the noise, and the confusion behind them.

When Felicity woke the next day, her room was so full of sunlight she knew it was long past noon. *Today is April twenty-first. It is my birthday*, she realized. *I am ten years old today. I wonder if it will be a happy day.* She stared at the bright path the sunshine made on her floor and thought about the dark events of the night before.

Felicity could hear the muffled bustle of her family going about household chores below her. Then her door opened a crack. Father looked in.

"Ah, you are awake," he said.

Felicity sat up. "Father," she said. "What happened? Did they catch the marines? Did they bring the gunpowder back?"

"No," said Father. "All is quiet now. The crowd was angry, though. The people marched over to the Palace early this morning to see the governor. They demanded that the governor return the gunpowder or pay for it." Mr. Merriman sighed. "But even if he does make amends, I am afraid none of us will trust the governor ever again. Nothing will be the same after the incident at the Magazine last night. Nothing will ever be the same."

"Father," said Felicity, "will you trust *me* again? Will you and Mother and Grandfather ever trust me again?"

"Well," said Mr. Merriman, "you made a terrible mistake, taking the guitar. But you made no mistake about the incident at the Magazine. You told the truth, and you acted bravely. I think you have earned back our trust."

"Will Grandfather forgive me?" asked Felicity.

"You will have to ask him that yourself," said Father. "All of this business has been very hard on your grandfather. He feels a great loyalty to his king, but he has lost faith in Governor Dunmore. He thinks the governor was wrong to have taken the gunpowder. 'Tis hard for an honorable gentleman like your grandfather when he loses his trust in someone he once respected." Mr. Merriman kissed Felicity's forehead. "Dress and come down to the parlor," he said as he left.

Felicity put on her pink gown and pinned a flowered apron over it. Grandfather would like the little posies on it. The spring sunshine had lit a tiny hope in her.

Perhaps spring's promise of the world starting anew would be true for her, and she could start anew with Grandfather. Perhaps Grandfather *would* forgive her.

When Felicity walked into the parlor, she smiled in delight. Her whole family and Ben were gathered around the table, smiling back at her.

"Oh . . . oh, it's enchanting!" Felicity gasped as she looked around the room. The parlor was transformed. Huge bunches of flowers made the room look like a garden in bloom.

At the center of it all was the table with Felicity's favorite plates and the glass pyramid laden with a cake and tarts. The silver chocolate pot gleamed like a mirror. It was surrounded by Mother's very finest pale yellow cups with their fancy handles. Felicity felt as if she were looking at a dream.

Mother kissed Felicity gently. Then she fastened a pompon of pretty pink, blue, and white flowers to Felicity's hair ribbon. "This is for you, my dear girl," she said, "with wishes for great happiness on your birthday."

"Thank you, Mother," said Felicity. She kissed her mother's cheek.

Grandfather came forward carrying the quintal vase filled with colorful flowers. In the center of the vase, Grandfather had placed the stubborn weed from Felicity's garden. It had blossomed into bright pink flowers. Felicity smiled when she saw it. Grandfather smiled, too.

"Aye, 'tis your weed," he said. "I decided something that is so determined to grow must be respected. And I think someone as brave as you must be forgiven a mistake."

Felicity hugged him as hard as she could.

"You were born this day ten years ago," Grandfather went on. "And with your birth began a joy unlike any other we'd ever known. We want to celebrate the joy you bring us, Felicity."

Grandfather reached into his pocket. He pulled out a long, wide, silk ribbon of a deep, shimmering red. "This is to replace the old ribbon on your guitar," he said. "I have decided that you should keep the guitar. I am sure you will treasure it now more than ever."

Felicity could hardly speak for happiness. "Oh, I will, Grandfather," she said. "I will."

# King's Creek Plantation

## CHAPTER 6

**F**elicity wanted to whoop for joy. She ran so fast she was almost flying. Down the wide stone steps she ran, down the gently sloping green lawn, and through the garden bright with flowers. She ran all the way to the edge of the bluff, and there she stopped.

Below her was the river, wide and blue and dazzling with light as it flowed along on its way to the sea. Felicity grinned. Every summer of her life she had come to stay at Grandfather's plantation on the York River. And every summer the very first thing she did when she arrived was run to the river. Summer did not begin until she'd seen the river's wide-open sweep and heard its welcoming murmur. *Hello, river,* Felicity thought. *Here I am, back again. What adventures do you have in store for me this summer?*

Grandfather's plantation was called King's Creek Plantation. It was about halfway between Williamsburg and Yorktown. Corn, wheat, and oats grew in the rolling fields above the riverbank. Cattle, sheep, and horses grazed in the sweet clover pastures. The fields, the slave quarters, and all the outbuildings of the plantation were on either side of the main house. Between the house and the river was a lawn flanked on both sides by dense woods. The lawn was green and broad. It was laced with white shell paths and decorated with flower beds.

Felicity turned from the river and saw Nan and William hurrying toward her along one of the paths. Mother and Grandfather strolled behind at a more gracious pace. Mother's parasol floated like a butterfly above the colorful flowers.

"Lissie," said Nan as she and William reached the riverbank, "I've brought your gathering basket. Grandfather says the first blackberries are ready to pick."

"Blackberries!" said William, all out of breath. "I'll eat the most!"

"Aye!" laughed Felicity. "And you shall most likely eat them before they're ever in your basket!"

"Felicity, do you remember where the best blackberry bushes are?" asked Grandfather with a twinkle in his eye.

"Indeed I do!" said Felicity. "They're in the thicket at the edge of the woods."

"Quite right," said Grandfather.

Felicity smiled at him. "You know I remember everything about King's Creek Plantation, Grandfather," she said.

"I believe you love it as much as I do," said Grandfather proudly.

Mother slipped her hand through the crook of Grandfather's elbow. "Off with you then, children," she said cheerfully. "Your grandfather and I will wait in the shade by the house while you gather blackberries for us."

Felicity grinned at Nan and William. "Let's race!" she said. The three children set off at a run toward the berry bushes.

"That's my Lissie," laughed Mother to Grandfather. "She's not here an hour and already she's running as wild as one of your colts!"

The bushes were thick with berries. In no time at all, Nan and Felicity had filled their baskets. William's basket was only half full, but he himself was covered with berry juice as dark as ink.

After the children washed their hands, they presented the berries to Grandfather and Mother. "Thank you!" said Grandfather. He popped a berry into his mouth. "These blackberries are fit for the king!"

"We have something else for you, too, Grandfather," said Felicity. She handed him a package. "It is a gift from Father's store." Mr. Merriman had stayed in Williamsburg to run his store with Ben to help him.

"Father let me choose it," said William. He watched impatiently as Grandfather unwrapped the package. "It's a bird bottle," William explained. "You put it on the side of a building, and birds build nests in it and eat any insects that come around."

"How very fine!" said Grandfather. "I thank you."

"Of course, birds build their nests in the spring, not the summer," said Nan in her sweetly serious voice. "There's no sense in putting up the bird bottle now. 'Tis the middle of July."

Felicity saw William's disappointed face. "Oh, but the birds will surely want to *visit* the bird bottle," she said quickly. Felicity turned to Grandfather. "I think we should put it up right away. Don't you, Grandfather?"

"Yes, indeed," said Grandfather. And so the three children helped Grandfather attach the bird bottle to the smokehouse, just under the eave of the roof.

When they were finished, Grandfather said, "There! Now perhaps I will have birds as well as children visiting this summer." He put his arm around Felicity's shoulders and smiled down at her. "All my visitors make me very happy."

That evening, while Nan, William, and Felicity were playing battledore and shuttlecock on the lawn, they saw a bird fluttering around the bird bottle. They stood quietly. The bird perched on the bottle, tilted his head, and studied them with his bright black eyes. He chirped mightily for a while, as if to proclaim his ownership of the bird bottle. Then he flew away.

"Why didn't he go inside the bird bottle?" asked William.

"He's probably too busy," Felicity answered. "He doesn't want to be indoors, anyway. There's too much to do out of doors."

That was certainly how Felicity felt. She loved summers at Grandfather's plantation because she could be out of doors almost all day long. It seemed to her that life on the plantation was busy and lazy at the same time. There were a great many things to do, all of them pleasant, and there was never any hurry about getting them done.

Felicity's days began early and peacefully. Every morning before dawn, Felicity and Grandfather met at the stable. Grandfather rode his old stallion, Major, and Felicity sat sidesaddle on a ladylike mare named Jessamine. Together they rode at an easy trot to the bluff above the river. There they waited for the sunrise.

The early morning was so still, Felicity thought she could almost hear the sun rising. It seemed to whisper as it slid smoothly up from behind the hills, warming the gray clouds to pink, the black hills to green, and the silvery river to blue. The sun filled the day with light and color.

"Well, now, Felicity my dear," Grandfather would say as they felt the sun on their faces, "let us put this day to good use." And they would gather their reins and turn their horses toward the fields.

Some mornings Felicity and Grandfather rode from one end of the plantation to the other, all the way from

King's Creek to the old footpath that led to Yorktown.
There was so much to see! Summer was a generous
season. Strawberries grew in thick clusters along the
edges of the fields. Fat watermelons and muskmelons
grew in the melon patch. Plump peaches, nectarines,
and figs grew in the orchard, just waiting to be plucked
and eaten. Lavender grew in the sunny herb garden.
The air was sweet with the smell of sun on flowers and
fruit.

While the morning was still cool, Felicity and
Grandfather inspected the green fields. She'd listen
while Grandfather spoke to the field hands and the
overseer about the weather. She'd let go of the reins
while Jessamine grazed with the sheep and cows in the
grassy meadows.

Most of all, Felicity loved to watch the horses running in the huge, fenced pasture. Grandfather loved
horses, too. He understood how Felicity felt when she
talked about Penny. "Whenever I see horses, I search
for Penny," Felicity said. "I never have stopped hoping that someday I will see Penny again. Do you think
that's being foolish, Grandfather?"

Grandfather shook his head. "No, my dear girl,"

he said. "I think that's being faithful."

When the morning grew warmer, Grandfather and Felicity would head back to the house through the woods. Grandfather would often stop to point out and name the wild herbs and other plants they passed.

"That's witch hazel," he said one day. "Its juice makes a good medicine to put on a bruise. If you gather some sprigs, we'll borrow the cook's mortar and pestle and I'll show you how to grind witch hazel to extract its juice."

Felicity slipped down from her saddle to pick sprigs of witch hazel and put them in her gathering basket.

One morning, Grandfather told Felicity about the times when he was a young man who had just arrived in Virginia from England. "I often went west on hunting trips," he said. "I lived alone in woods like these for days."

"But where did you sleep?" asked Felicity. "What did you eat?"

"Fallen trees gave me shelter. Pine boughs were my bed," answered Grandfather. "I hunted birds and game. I ate roots and berries. 'Twas a fine, simple life."

"It sounds so adventurous!" said Felicity. She

imagined living in the cool, dark woods, under a fallen tree, where she would be surrounded by the smell of rich, damp earth. How wonderful to be so wild and free!

"The earth is happy to provide us with everything we need," said Grandfather as they left their horses at the stable. "We must only be wise enough to know how to use it."

# Faithful Friends

## CHAPTER 7

The serene and sunny summer days flowed by as smoothly as the river. By the end of July, Felicity was completely settled into the rhythm of life on the plantation. She often thought of her father, and Ben, and Elizabeth back home in Williamsburg. She missed them not because she was lonely, but because she wanted to share with them all the good times and quiet delights of summer at King's Creek Plantation.

One hot afternoon, Felicity and William were playing by the river in Grandfather's boat, which was pulled partway onto the shore. William was pretending to row. The family had rowed upriver to a barbecue and boat race the day before, and William was now determined to be a boatman. Felicity had a shell full of soapy water. She dipped a hollow reed in it and blew bubbles, and then watched the bubbles drift lazily up toward the clouds.

The sun was as heavy as a weight on Felicity's back. But she had taken off her shoes and stockings so that she could dangle her legs over the end of the boat and dip her toes into the river water. And her wide-brimmed straw hat shaded her face, so Felicity felt perfectly comfortable.

Nan appeared at the top of the bluff. She waved and called out as she ran down to them, "Lissie! William! 'Tis time for dinner."

William quickly climbed out of the boat. He was always interested in dinner. But Felicity sighed as she pulled her feet out of the water. She was always sorry to go inside.

"Lissie!" giggled Nan when she got to the boat. "Gracious me! Hurry and put on your shoes and stockings. Mr. and Mrs. Wentworth are here to visit. It wouldn't be proper for guests to see you bare-legged!"

Felicity sighed again as she put on her shoes and stockings. "I wish we had no guests today," she said. "I'd rather stay out of doors."

There were very often guests for dinner. Ladies and gentlemen from all the neighboring plantations came to call on Mother. She had grown up here on Grandfather's plantation, and all her old friends were eager to see her. Felicity liked it very much when families with children visited. All the children had dinner by themselves, separately from the adults. They ate their dinner quickly and then were free to go out of doors. They went for walks or played battledore and shuttlecock on the lawn. But when there were no children visiting, Felicity ate with the adults. Nan and William ate in the kitchen. It was considered a privilege to be allowed to join the adults in the dining room. But it did not feel like a privilege when Mrs. Wentworth was one of the dinner guests. Felicity feared it would be a dull afternoon.

And indeed, Mrs. Wentworth had a great deal to say at dinnertime. "Well!" she exclaimed. "When I heard that Governor Dunmore and his family had left Williamsburg, I quite nearly went into spasms! Governor Dunmore was sent to the colonies by the king himself to govern us. If he must flee from his Palace, then none of us is safe! We shall all be murdered in our beds by these wild Patriots! They are disloyal to our king!" She turned to her husband, who appeared to be dozing. "Don't you agree, Mr. Wentworth?" she asked sharply.

"What? Oh! Yes, indeed, my dear," said Mr. Wentworth.

"Think of it!" Mrs. Wentworth went on. "The governor and his family were forced to stay on a ship in Norfolk! I hear Lady Dunmore and the children are now sailing safely home to England!" Mrs. Wentworth's plumpish face was pink as a boiled ham. "I'm simply scandalized! I'm glad you're far from Williamsburg this summer, my dear Mrs. Merriman. And your dear sweet children! Do you not fear for your husband? And you in your condition, too!"

Felicity saw her mother blush. Mother was expecting a baby in the winter. "My dear Mrs. Wentworth," Mother said calmly, "do not upset yourself. 'Tis true, the governor and his family left Williamsburg. Relations between the governor and the colonists were no longer friendly. But 'twas a peaceful departure. No one wished the governor or his family any harm. As for my husband . . . " Mother smiled. "I've no fear for him.

He is a sensible, peaceful man. He keeps a cool head."

Mrs. Wentworth waggled *her* head. "Well!" she went on. "All this trouble began in November, when those hot-headed Patriots threw crates of tea into this very river, just down the road in Yorktown. 'Twas then that so many merchants decided to stop selling tea in their shops. They stopped because they were too disloyal to pay the king's tax on it! Scandalous, if you ask me."

No one *had* asked Mrs. Wentworth. In fact, no one had said anything at all. Felicity, Mother, and Grandfather were awkwardly silent because Felicity's father was one of the merchants who had stopped selling tea in his store. He had stopped because he believed the king's tax was unfair, not because he was disloyal.

Felicity glanced at Grandfather. She knew he thought Father was wrong not to sell tea. But Grandfather was too polite to say anything that would make Mother uncomfortable in front of the Wentworths. *'Tis a good thing Ben is not here,* Felicity thought. Ben was a Patriot, heart and soul. He'd be sure to say something that would send Mrs. Wentworth into spasms.

The dining room was hot and stuffy, and Mrs. Wentworth's words only made it worse. Felicity knew she should sit still and appear to be interested in the conversation even though she did not like what Mrs. Wentworth was saying. But her feet were jumpy, and her legs itched. There was sand stuck in her stockings. Felicity put her hands through the slits in her gown and petticoat as if she were reaching into her pockets. She slipped her hands past her pockets, untied her garters, and put them in her pockets. Then she jiggled her legs so that her stockings fell down around her ankles. Ah, now, *that* felt better!

"Gracious!" said Mrs. Wentworth suddenly.

Felicity realized Mrs. Wentworth was looking at her.

"Felicity!" Mrs. Wentworth puffed. "You are as twitchy as a cat's tail! What ails you, child?"

Quickly, Felicity put her hands up on the table. "Well, I . . . " she began.

Grandfather rescued her. "May I ask you ladies to excuse the gentlemen?" he asked. "Mr. Wentworth has brought some horses for me to look at. And I would like Felicity to join us. I shall need her advice. She has quite an eye for a good horse."

"Oh, yes, of course!" said Mother. Mrs. Wentworth nodded.

Felicity was so grateful to be going, she forgot about her stockings. They flopped around her ankles as she followed the gentlemen out of doors and down the path to the pasture behind the stable. The sun was scorching hot. Still, it felt wonderful to be out of doors.

Felicity took a deep breath. She loved the stable smell of horses and sun-warmed hay. She stood next to Grandfather and looked over the pasture fence at the five horses Mr. Wentworth had brought. Most of the horses stood quietly in the shade of the stable, nibbling at the grass. Felicity shaded her eyes to better see one horse that was at the far end of the pasture, trotting restlessly along the fence.

"These are cart horses," Mr. Wentworth said to Grandfather. "Some of them are handsome enough to pull your riding chair. The others are steady and strong. You won't find a better horse than one of these to pull a farm wagon."

"They appear to be in fine condition," said Grandfather. "Let's have a closer look." He opened the gate and led Felicity and Mr. Wentworth into the pasture.

The stable boys looped ropes around the horses' necks and led them to Grandfather one by one. Grandfather inspected the horses carefully. He ran his hands down their legs and looked at their eyes and teeth to be sure the horses were healthy.

Suddenly, there was an uproar. The horse at the far end of the pasture whinnied, and kicked up its heels, and ran wildly. It would not let the stable boy near enough to put the rope around its neck.

Mr. Wentworth shook his head. "That horse was passed along to me in a swap and I took her, for she's a Thoroughbred," he said. "She's handsome, and fast as the very wind. But she's very skittish. I fear she was once so badly mistreated, she trusts no one."

The horse reared up, and Felicity gasped. She slipped past Grandfather and ran toward the horse as fast as she could.

"Stop!" Mr. Wentworth shouted. "Stop! That horse is dangerous!"

The horse was skinny and scruffy and so covered with dust that her coat was the color of mud. She tossed her head and danced from side to side. Felicity made herself slow to a walk as she came nearer. Her heart thudded in her chest so that she could hardly breathe.

"Penny," Felicity said softly. "Penny. It's me. It's Felicity. You remember. You remember me, don't you, Penny? Don't you, my girl?" Felicity stood still and held out her hands. "Come to me, Penny," she said. "Come, my fine one."

The horse nickered. She took one step, then two, toward Felicity. Then, very gently, she nudged Felicity's shoulder with her nose.

Felicity's eyes filled with happy tears. She reached up and put her arms around Penny's neck. "I knew we would find each other again someday," Felicity whispered.

Felicity turned and slowly walked back toward Grandfather. Penny followed close behind her. The men stood by the stable, watching, silent. Felicity smiled at Grandfather. "This is my horse, Grandfather," Felicity said simply. "This is Penny."

Grandfather's gray eyes shone with happiness. He cleared his throat. Then he said to Mr. Wentworth, "I'll take this horse along with the others, if you'd be so kind." He shook hands with Mr. Wentworth to seal the bargain.

"I've never seen such a thing in all my days," said Mr. Wentworth. "It does my heart good to know that horse has found a home." He turned to Felicity. "You're a brave young lady," he said. "You deserve a horse as spirited as this."

"She does indeed," said Grandfather. "She does indeed."

That night, Felicity took paper from the leather pocketbook Father had given her. She wrote a letter to Father and Ben to tell them about Penny. She knew Ben would be happy, because he had shared her secret about taming Penny last autumn. That had been the beginning of her friendship with Ben.

Then Felicity wrote:

> *30 July 1775*
> *My Dear Friend Elizabeth,*
>
> *I pray this letter finds you in good Health and good spirits. Such great Happiness is mine! Today, my dear horse Penny is returned to me. Grandfather has purchased her. I am to care for her while I am here. All this afternoon I have spent with her,*

*brushing and currying her. She is thin, but in good Health. My Joy is twice as great, because I know you share it with me. You hoped for Penny's return as much as I did, and never let me lose Faith. Tonight my Heart is full of Happiness, and full of Love for you. I am, and shall be forever,*

    *Your faithful Friend,*
*Felicity Merriman*

# The Note in the Bird Bottle

## CHAPTER 8

**D**uring the months they had been apart, Felicity had often imagined what it would be like if she were ever with Penny again. But even in her dreams, she had not imagined how happy she would feel, or how content. It was as if something sad and longing in her had finally come to peace, all because Penny was back.

"I have never seen two living creatures so glad to be with one another," said Grandfather. He and Mother were watching Felicity make medicine to put on a scrape on Penny's leg.

"Aye," agreed Mother. "Indeed, 'tis a pleasure to see."

Felicity ground herbs with the pestle to make a smooth mixture. Then she scooped up some with her fingers and spread it on Penny's scrape. "The wound is healing well, Grandfather," she said.

"You have done a fine job of caring for that horse," said Grandfather. "She looks like a different animal entirely from the wild creature that she was two weeks ago. She's filled out, and her coat is as shiny as a . . . "

"Bright copper penny!" Felicity said. "Isn't Penny a love, Grandfather? She's so fast! And did you see how well she accepted the sidesaddle? She took to it better than I did myself!"

"You do look like a fine lady upon her, Lissie, my dear," said Mother. "I wish your friend Elizabeth could see you. She would be so happy."

Felicity felt a tiny prick of sorrow. Elizabeth had sent her a lovely letter saying how happy she was that Penny was with Felicity again. But Felicity did not know if Elizabeth would ever see her with Penny. Penny was to stay on Grandfather's plantation when Mother and the children returned to Williamsburg at the end of August. After all, Grandfather owned her. Besides, if Felicity brought Penny back to Williamsburg, it might be dangerous. There was no telling what Mr. Nye would do. He was the man who had claimed to own Penny last fall. He had beaten and starved her.

He might steal Penny away and hurt her again.

But for now, Mr. Nye was far away, and Felicity spent every minute she could with her beloved horse. When she and Grandfather rode in the mornings, Penny was well behaved. She followed Grandfather's horse obediently and never fought the slow, steady pace. Their morning rides were such a pleasure, Felicity and Grandfather made them longer. Sometimes they followed the footpath as far as Philgate's Creek. Once, they even crossed the creek and rode all the way to where the path split. One fork led to a little finger of land that stuck out into the river, called Sandy Point. The other fork led to Yorktown.

After dinner, when Nan and William played and Grandfather and Mother rested, Felicity rode Penny to the huge upper pasture. The grass seemed to shimmer with heat, and the air was so dense and hot it felt solid. Felicity would lean forward and whisper, "Run, Penny, as fast as you like." Penny would walk, then trot, then canter. Faster and faster Penny would fly, smooth as water, while Felicity held on tight, and the whole world was a brilliant blur around them.

One steamy afternoon, as Felicity was riding Penny

from the stable to the upper pasture for their canter, she passed Nan and William. They had reeds, and shells full of soapy water, and they were blowing bubbles up into the branches of a large, old shade tree.

"Lissie," said William, "when you pass the bird bottle, do remember to look inside it. Maybe a bird has built a nest today."

Felicity and Nan looked at each other and sighed. William asked Felicity to look in the bird bottle almost every day, even though both girls had told him a hundred times that birds don't build nests in the summer. "William," said Nan patiently, "you and Lissie looked yesterday. There is no nest in the bottle. There never is. There never is *anything* in the bottle."

William ignored Nan. "You'll look, won't you, Lissie? Promise?"

"I promise," said Felicity quickly. She was impatient to go. She nudged Penny, and they trotted away. As they passed the smokehouse, Felicity glanced at the bird bottle to keep her promise to William, even though she knew nothing would be there.

But to her great surprise, Felicity saw something white in the bird bottle. She reined Penny to a stop and squinted at it. Was the sun playing tricks on her eyes? Felicity rode up for a closer look.

There *was* something there. It was a scrap of cloth. Felicity put her hand in the bird bottle and pulled the cloth out. It looked like the corner of a handkerchief. It was wrapped around something hard, something like a stick. Quickly, Felicity unrolled the cloth. Out fell a wooden whistle. Felicity stared at it. She knew it was a signal whistle because she had seen Ben's. He had shown her how to blow it, and how it was used to give commands to soldiers. In fact, this signal whistle looked exactly like Ben's. Whose was it? Why had someone put it in the bird bottle? Why was it wrapped in a scrap of handkerchief that was stained with berry juice?

Felicity looked at the stains more closely and gasped. They were not stains at all! They were words, written with a stick dipped in berry juice! Felicity read the words on the scrap of cloth:

> *Felicity, Come! Help!*
> *Ben*

Ben? Ben was supposed to be in Williamsburg. How

could he have left this note for her? Where was he? If he was nearby, why didn't he come to the house? And why did he need her help? Felicity's mind was spinning.

Below the words on the scrap of cloth, Ben had made a rough map. The map showed Grandfather's house, the river, and the woods. There was an X in the woods. That must be where Ben was.

Felicity took a shaky breath. Suddenly, it was all clear to her. Ben was hiding. For some reason, he didn't want anyone but her to know where he was. Ben wanted her to find him by following the map. She should blow his signal whistle so that he would know it was safe to show himself. Felicity did not stop to think anymore. She urged Penny to a trot and went to look for Ben in the woods.

Felicity and Penny entered the woods just behind the blackberry thicket. When they were deep in the forest, Felicity blew the signal whistle once, twice, three times. She heard Ben whistle in reply, and she rode toward the sound. It was not hard to find him, though he was well away from the riding path. He sat propped up against a big tree. One leg was stretched out in front of him, wrapped in bloody rags.

"Ben!" exclaimed Felicity. "Benjamin Davidson! What on earth are you doing here?" She slipped off Penny's back. "What's happened to you?"

Ben groaned and closed his eyes. Felicity stopped talking. She knelt next to him and then said quietly, "Ben, tell me what you are doing."

Ben opened his eyes. His face was sweaty and streaked with mud. "I ran away," he said. "You know I want to be a soldier and fight with the Patriots. Two companies of soldiers from Virginia have already marched to Massachusetts to join the army George Washington is gathering there." Ben took a deep breath. "It's starting, Lissie," he said. "General Washington is going to lead an army of Patriots. We're going to fight the British. We're going to overthrow the rule of the king here in the colonies. I want to be part of the fight. But my apprenticeship agreement with your father won't allow it. So," he repeated, "I ran away."

"When?" asked Felicity.

"The night before last," answered Ben. "I thought I could make it to the Yorktown ferry and cross the river before your father . . . before I was missed."

Felicity sighed. "What went wrong?" she asked.

"I knew I couldn't walk along the main road for fear of being seen," said Ben. "Still, I made good time through the woods until I came to King's Creek. It was so dark, I slipped and fell when I was crossing the creek. I lost my pack of clothes and food and money. And I cut my leg on a sharp branch."

"Your leg looks bad," said Felicity. "It must hurt."

Ben shrugged. "I knew I was not far from your Grandfather's plantation, and I knew I needed your help. I found my way here and slept by this tree. Yesterday, I sneaked up closer to the house. I saw you and William looking at the bird bottle. So last night, I wrote you that message and hid it with my whistle in the bird bottle. I was hoping you'd find them today. I am very glad you did."

"I'm glad, too," said Felicity. She stood up and dusted off her gown. "Because now I can tell you how foolish I think you're being. I'm going straight up to the house to fetch Grandfather."

Ben reached up and grabbed Felicity's arm. "Don't!" he said. "Your grandfather is a Loyalist. He thinks the Patriots are wrong. You can't tell him about me, Lissie!"

Felicity yanked her arm away. "Yes, I can!" she said. "I'd be dishonest if I didn't. I can't keep a secret like this!" She stalked away and swung herself up onto Penny.

"Lissie," said Ben softly, "that's Penny, isn't it? I got your letter, saying that she was here. You must be happy to have your horse back."

"Yes!" said Felicity, "I—" Suddenly, she stopped. She looked down at Ben. He was solemn. Felicity remembered how Ben had helped her keep Penny a secret last fall. Ben had never told Mother or Father that Felicity was sneaking off every morning to ride Penny. She had asked Ben to keep her secret, and he had. How could she not do the same for him?

Felicity spoke slowly. "Very well, Ben," she said. "I promise I will not tell anyone about you. You can trust me. I'll go back to the house now. But I'll be back soon with food and water and some medicine for your leg. Rest easy. I won't be long." She smiled at Ben a little bit. "You kept my secret. I shall keep yours. I promise."

Ben grinned for the first time. "I knew you would, Felicity," he said. "You are a faithful friend."

# Runaway

*T*he afternoon sun was shining strong on the pines, and the air was scented with piney tang when Felicity returned to Ben in the woods. She handed Ben a basket of food. "You look as though you need this," she said.

Ben took the food gratefully. "Indeed I do!" he said. "I've eaten enough blackberries to fill twenty pies, but I am still hungry!"

"You'll need your strength," said Felicity. She knelt next to him. "I'm going to look at your leg." Very gently, Felicity unwrapped the rags from around Ben's leg. They were stiff with dried blood. Underneath them, Felicity saw a jagged gash running from the ankle to the knee. She washed the cut with river water she'd brought. "Now I'm going to put medicine on your leg," she told Ben. "It may hurt a bit."

Ben concentrated on the bread he was eating. He only flinched a bit at the medicine's sting. "How do you know so much about medicine?" he asked.

"Grandfather taught me," said Felicity. "He showed me how to grind herbs to make this medicine for Penny. It helped her scrape heal. It should help you, too."

Felicity wrapped Ben's leg in strips from a clean petticoat. She tied the bandage with a ribbon.

Ben smiled when he looked at the ribbon. "Well, my leg certainly looks prettier," he said. "It feels better, too."

"It will be as good as new in a week or so," said Felicity.

"A week!" exclaimed Ben. "I can't wait here that long!"

Felicity shrugged. "You have no choice. Besides," she said briskly, "I can't see that a sickly, skinny, limping soldier would do General Washington and his army one bit of good." She stood up and began to gather pine boughs from a fallen tree to make a bed for Ben.

"Felicity," said Ben. "What do you think about all this—about General Washington and his army of Patriots?"

"I'm sorry the disagreements between the king and the colonists have gone so far," said Felicity. "I hoped there wouldn't be any fighting. I hoped the differences could be solved another way."

"That's what your father says," said Ben. "So you agree with him. You think I am wrong."

Felicity sat down and looked straight at Ben. "Aye," she said. "I can't say you are wrong to stand up for what you believe in. But I do think you are going about it the wrong way. Breaking your apprenticeship agreement with my father is not honorable. It's wrong the way a lie is wrong. You'll shame your family and yourself. I'm afraid—"

"*I'm* not afraid," Ben cut in. "If you were older, you'd understand."

"Oh!" said Felicity tartly. "Well! I understand enough to know that this is not a brave beginning! If you run away from my father, what will happen when you meet an enemy?"

Ben was quiet.

"Did you even talk to my father?" Felicity asked. "Did you even ask him to let you go?"

Ben frowned. "You know as well as I do that he

would hold me to my apprenticeship agreement," he said. "Your father would not let me break my promise to him."

"Indeed," said Felicity slowly. "I always thought it was a promise you made to yourself, to do what you said you would do, no matter how hard it was."

Ben leaned his head back against the tree.

Felicity stood up. "I'm going now," she said. "But I will be back tomorrow. I hope you'll think about what we've said."

"I will," said Ben. "But I will not change my mind."

"No," said Felicity, "but maybe you will have a change of heart."

It was not difficult for Felicity to visit Ben the next few days, nor was it difficult to find food for him. The cook never minded if Felicity took food from the kitchen, and it was easy to gather berries and peaches still warm from the sun. Felicity put to use some of the things Grandfather had taught her about living in the woods to make Ben more comfortable. The medicine was helping Ben's leg heal quickly. In fact, Felicity did not want to tell Ben how well his leg was healing. She kept hoping he might decide not to go. But the decision was forced upon him sooner than she expected.

One morning, as Felicity, Nan, William, and Grandfather were eating breakfast, Mother came into the dining room and handed Grandfather a letter. Then she turned to the children and said, "The letter is from your father, children. He is coming here tomorrow, rather than waiting until Sunday as usual."

"Hurray!" said Nan and William.

Felicity wished she could feel as happy as they did. But she couldn't. She thought she knew why Father was coming. He was looking for Ben. She made her voice sound calm. "Oh! How fine," she said.

Grandfather put the letter down and said crisply, "It seems that Ben, that hot-headed apprentice, has run off. I warned your father about Ben when I was in Williamsburg this spring. I said he was spending too much time watching the militia muster. Now it appears I was right. That foolish boy has run off—probably to fight with the Patriots. Humph! Your father is well rid of such a troublesome scoundrel."

"Now, now," said Mother. "Ben's a good lad.

Maybe he's gone to visit his family and plans to come back."

"Well!" said Grandfather. "Then why did he leave without a word? And why did your husband put a notice in the *Gazette*?"

"Father put a notice in the newspaper?" asked Felicity.

"Here it is," said Grandfather. "You may have it."

Felicity's eyes widened with fear as she read:

> WILLIAMSBURG, *August 19, 1775*
> *Run away from the Subscriber, on the 15th*
> *Day of August, an APPRENTICE Lad*
> *named BENJAMIN DAVIDSON, 6 feet high,*
> *about 16 years old, slender and well made,*
> *of a clear complexion, has long brown hair,*
> *brown eyes, a forthright look, and frank*
> *manner. I have reason to believe he is headed*
> *Yorktown way. Whoever delivers the said*
> *Apprentice to me shall have eight dollars*
> *Reward; and I hearby forewarn all persons*
> *not to harbour or entertain him.*
> $\qquad\qquad\qquad$ *EDWARD MERRIMAN*

Felicity excused herself and hurried to her bed-
chamber. She sat at the open window and looked out
across the long lawn. She could see the river flowing
along to the sea. It never stopped. It never wavered. The
river was always so sure of its course. But Felicity was
not. She did not know what to do. She looked down at
the notice in her hand. "I hereby forewarn all persons
not to harbour or entertain him," Father had written. By
caring for Ben and helping him hide, Felicity was doing
exactly what Father said *not* to do.

When Father arrived, should she tell him about
Ben? Felicity sighed. She wished she could tell Father.
But she had made a promise to Ben, and she knew she
had to keep it. Felicity took a piece of paper out of her
pocketbook. She began to draw a map of the route from
Grandfather's plantation to Yorktown. She would help
Ben run away, even though she did not want him to go.

Felicity held her pocketbook to her chest as she
ran to the woods. A storm was coming. The wind was
fitful, and the air was yellowish green. Her hair was
wild and she was out of breath when she reached Ben.
"Ben!" she said. "Father is coming. He's put a notice
in the *Gazette* about you and offered a reward for your

return. Will you stay and talk to him?"

"No," said Ben, just as Felicity had expected.

"Then you had better leave right away," said Felicity. "Come, stand up and follow me. I'll show you the path to Yorktown. Hurry."

Ben said not a word as he stood up. He winced as he put his weight on his injured leg, and he wobbled a bit when he tried to walk.

"Here," said Felicity. "Lean on me. You can do it."

Felicity supported Ben as they made their way through the woods along the footpath. She and Grandfather had ridden along the path many times, so Felicity was sure of the way. But she and Ben moved very slowly. The path was narrow, and bumpy with tree roots. Ben struggled and stumbled. It felt like hours before they reached Philgate's Creek. Felicity helped Ben across, wading through the shallow water. They rested a minute on the far shore. Then Felicity handed Ben her pocketbook.

"I'm going back now," she said. "Take this. There's a map inside to show you the rest of the way to Yorktown. And I've put money in it, too. It's not much, but it should pay your fare on the ferry to Gloucester. Be sure to follow my map. Stay on the path. Don't take the main road or . . . " Felicity hesitated, "or there may be trouble."

Ben nodded. "Good-bye, Lissie," he said. "Thank you. I won't forget you."

Felicity was too sad to speak. She watched Ben's back until it disappeared, swallowed up in the mouth of a leafy tunnel. She wondered if she'd ever see Ben again. A fat raindrop hit her shoulder, and she turned to go.

It was almost noon and the rain was steady when Felicity got back to the house. As she came inside, Felicity heard unfamiliar voices in the parlor. *Probably guests for dinner,* she thought. She began to go up the stairs to her chamber. She stopped dead still when she heard one of the voices say, "Don't you worry, sir. We'll find the apprentice lad and bring him back if we have to drag him!"

Felicity sat down hard. Another voice, even rougher than the first one, said, "As soon as we saw Mr. Merriman's notice, my partner and me, we didn't waste no time. We set out to find the runaway."

"Well, I can assure you the lad is not anywhere on

my plantation," said Grandfather. "Someone would
have seen him."

"All right, sir. If you say so, sir," said the first man.
"We'll be on our way to Yorktown then. We'll ask at the
ferry if he went across the river to Gloucester. If he did,
we'll follow him."

*The ferry!* thought Felicity in a panic. That was
exactly where Ben was headed! If they left now, and
took the main road, these men would get to the ferry
before Ben would. Ben would walk straight into a trap!

"We've dealt with runaways before, sir," the second
man was saying. "We ain't afraid to be rough if needs
be."

Felicity did not hear what Grandfather replied. She
was up and away, out the door, running to the stable
through the rain. She had to stop Ben. She had to find
him before those men did.

# Penny Saves the Day

ﾐ CHAPTER 10 ﾐ

**F**elicity did not stop to saddle Penny. She slipped the bridle over Penny's head, led her from the stable, climbed up on the pasture fence, and swung herself onto Penny's back. Then she leaned forward and whispered to Penny, "This is not going to be easy, Penny my girl. The footpath will be slippery in this rain. But you must help me find Ben. I know we can do it."

The storm grew angrier and the rain fell harder as Penny carried Felicity into the woods. Wet branches waved around them wildly. They looked like long green arms warning *turn back! turn back!* Felicity was blinded by the rain. She leaned low over Penny's neck and trusted Penny to find the way. Penny never faltered. Thunder crashed, making Felicity's heart jump. Lightning ripped the sky with sharp, wicked slashes. Through it all, Penny kept on in an easy canter, though the path was slick. Felicity knew Penny sensed her fear and urgency, but Penny was calm. It was as if she had turned all her willfulness and spirit to one task: helping Felicity find Ben.

When they came to Philgate's Creek, Penny jumped over the churning water in one smooth arch. Felicity whispered to her, "That's my girl. That's my Penny." Then on through the rain they rode.

Just past the turnoff for Sandy Point, Penny slowed. Felicity looked up and saw Ben scrambling into the woods, trying to hide.

"Ben! Stop!" she cried. "It's me!"

Ben turned. "Felicity!" he gasped, as Penny came toward him. "Why are you here?"

"Listen to me, Ben," said Felicity. She took a deep breath and then spilled the whole story in a rush. "When I got back to Grandfather's, two men were there. They had seen Father's notice in the newspaper. They are after you for the reward. They said they'd be rough with you, and I believe them. They are on their way to Yorktown now. They are going straight to the ferry, so they would be sure to catch you and probably beat you and drag you back." Felicity leaned toward Ben. "Can't you see how dangerous and foolish this running away is, Ben? Wouldn't you rather face Father than those two men? Come back with me now. Come back. Please."

Ben shook his head. "I can't," he said. "That would be cowardly."

Felicity was furious. She said just what she thought Grandfather would say. "You *are* a coward, Ben Davidson," she said. "It's cowardly to run away, to break promises, and to hurt those who need you and trust you. Now, will you come back?"

Ben was quiet. He put his hand on Penny's neck. She did not shy away. Then Ben said, "Will Penny let me ride her?"

Felicity smiled. "She will if I ask her to," she said.

"Indeed," Ben grinned. "It is hard to refuse you, Felicity Merriman."

The wind had calmed and the rain was falling more gently as Penny carried Felicity and Ben back through the woods. It was as if the storm had worn itself out with its fury and was now tired and weepy. Felicity was tired, too. She thought Penny must be, as well, though the horse walked on at a steady pace. Felicity patted Penny's neck. What a fine, brave horse she was!

Felicity had to leave behind her tiredness and gather all the bravery she could muster when she led Ben into the parlor to face Mother and Grandfather. Grandfather's face went white with anger when he saw Ben. His gray eyes were hard as gunmetal. He said nothing.

But Mother stood and smiled a small smile. "Ben," she said. "I am so glad you have . . . I am so glad you are here."

"Ben has decided not to run away," said Felicity. "He has been hiding in the woods by the river. I've been—I've been helping him. I'm sorry. I knew it was wrong, but I had to. Today I showed him the footpath to Yorktown. But then those men came, and I was afraid they would hurt Ben. So I followed him and . . . and . . ."

Ben spoke up. "Felicity convinced me not to go," he said. "She brought me back." He glanced at Grandfather and then said to Mother, "I am very sorry I ran away."

"Aye, indeed," said Mother quickly. "We will have time enough for apologies when Mr. Merriman comes. But now I daresay 'twould be best for both of you to find dry clothes. Come with me."

They were almost out the door when Grandfather called, "Felicity!"

Felicity turned around. "Yes, Grandfather?" she said softly.

"The lad says 'twas you who convinced him to come back," said Grandfather. "I am curious. How did you do it?"

"Well," said Felicity. She thought back over the things she had said to Ben. Then she remembered what had convinced him to change his mind. "I just said to him exactly what I thought *you* would have said, Grandfather."

"Humph!" said Grandfather. "Did you indeed?" He almost smiled. "Go along, then," he said. "You're as wet as if you'd jumped into the river."

After an early supper, Felicity went to her bed-chamber. She lay in bed listening to the night music the crickets and frogs made. A warm wind blew the soothing murmur of the river up to her. The storm that day had been violent, but like most violent storms, it was short. It left the air washed clean and sweet. Felicity fell asleep, worn out by her adventures.

When Father arrived in the morning, Felicity was
at breakfast. Ben was still asleep, and Mother said not
to wake him. So Felicity led Father to the stable to visit
Penny.

"Father," Felicity said. "I was wrong to help Ben run
away and not to tell anybody. And I am sorry. But I had
to keep his secret." She stroked Penny's neck. "Because
Ben kept my secret about Penny last autumn."

"I understand," said Father. He looked at Penny.
"Penny is a beautiful horse. You're glad to have her
back, aren't you, Lissie?"

"Aye," said Felicity. She hugged Penny. "And I am
glad she is safe from the likes of Mr. Nye."

"Everyone is safe from Jiggy Nye for the present,"
said Father. "When I left Williamsburg, Jiggy Nye was
in jail." Father looked at Felicity. "You'll miss Penny
when you leave here to go back to Williamsburg,
won't you?"

"Aye," said Felicity again, slowly. "But it won't be
as bad as it was before, when I helped Penny run away
and I didn't know whether I'd ever see her again. I
know where she is now."

"You know she's safe," agreed Father. "Maybe that

will make it a little easier to say good-bye. But," he sighed, "I'm afraid it's never very easy to say good-bye to friends we love."

"No," said Felicity. "But sometimes saying good-bye isn't the end of a friendship. I said good-bye to Penny when I let her go, but she came back."

"That she did," agreed Father.

Felicity looked at him very seriously. "I've been thinking about Ben," she said. "You could let him go be a soldier, Father. The fighting won't last forever. You could trust Ben to come back to you when the fighting is over. I know you could trust him."

Father did not answer, but Felicity knew he was thinking about what she had said.

In a little while, Ben appeared in the doorway of the stable. "I have come to apologize, Mr. Merriman," said Ben. "I'm sorry. 'Twas wrong to run away. I meant no disrespect to you, sir. You have always treated me well and fairly. But . . . " Ben squared his shoulders. "I do want to be a soldier."

Mr. Merriman stared at Ben for a while. Then he said, "I will not allow you to break your apprenticeship agreement with me, Ben. You are but sixteen. You are pledged to me for three more years. I expect you to give me three more years of service."

Ben nodded sadly.

Mr. Merriman went on slowly. "But in a little more than a year, you will be eighteen. If at that time you still wish to be a soldier, and if there is still such a thing as the Patriots' army, then I will let you go. But we must have the understanding that you will come back and finish out your service to me when your days of being a soldier are over. Does that seem fair to you?"

Ben's face brightened. "Yes, sir," he said. "Thank you, sir."

Father smiled at Felicity, and then turned to shake Ben's hand. "Good lad," he said. "I know that I can trust you."

"Aye, sir," said Ben. "You can."

All too soon, the sad day came when Felicity and her family had to return to Williamsburg. That last morning, Felicity and Grandfather rode out to see the sunrise together one more time. Felicity watched a branch bobbing along in the river. It sailed by, carried on the current, and soon disappeared from sight on its way to the sea. Grandfather watched it, too.

"Felicity," Grandfather said, "the world is changing. 'Tis changing too fast for an old man like me to keep up with it." He smiled at Felicity. "But how can I mind growing older, when I can watch you growing up, becoming a fine young lady, full of strength and wisdom and love."

Then Grandfather chuckled. "Indeed, many things are too fast for an old man like me," he said. "Especially that horse of yours. What am I to do with such a fast horse? I can't catch her, and she wouldn't let me ride her even if I could catch her. I think you had better take Penny back to Williamsburg with you. Your father tells me that Jiggy Nye is in jail, so she will be safe. Will you take good care of Penny for me?"

"Oh, yes, Grandfather!" exclaimed Felicity. "Thank you! I will! Oh, I truly will." Felicity was trembling, she was so happy.

"Very well, then," said Grandfather. He gathered up his reins. "Come along. You've a great deal to say good-bye to this morning."

Felicity gave Penny a quick hug. Then she gathered

her reins, too, and followed Grandfather to the fields. The plantation had never looked more lovely. But Felicity could think about only one thing: *Penny was going home with her!*

After breakfast, there were many hugs, kisses, thank-yous, and good-byes. Then Mother, Nan, Ben, and William climbed into the carriage. Father and Felicity rode beside them on their horses. Felicity sat tall and proud on Penny's back. She wished she could gallop all the way back to Williamsburg. She couldn't wait to show Penny to Elizabeth. But just as they reached the end of the lane, Felicity stopped. She turned around and looked back. Grandfather was standing on the steps of his house. He looked very small, almost lost in the shadows of the trees.

"Wait for me, Father," said Felicity. She urged Penny into a fast canter and rode back to Grandfather. When she reached him, Felicity jumped off Penny and ran to give Grandfather one last hug.

Felicity climbed back on Penny and hurried to join her family. She felt a sweet sadness at leaving this place that was so dear to her. But she rode on, into the sunshine ahead.

# A Cardinal
# and a Bluebird

## CHAPTER 11

**S**ummer passed, and then fall. Felicity rode Penny whenever she could. Soon it was winter. One bright January afternoon, after the holidays were over, the girls were playing with their dolls in the Merrimans' sunny garden.

"Would you like another tart?" Felicity asked Elizabeth. "Yes, thank you, Miss Merriman," said Elizabeth politely. She took two of the brown twigs Felicity offered her, one for herself and one for her doll, Charlotte. "You do make the most elegantly delicious tarts."

"That's kind of you to say, Miss Cole," said Felicity with a grin. "But I'm afraid these tarts are overdone." She snapped a twig in two with a *crack*.

"I like crisp tarts," laughed Elizabeth, "and so does Charlotte."

"Upon my word!" said a voice. The girls looked up

and saw Felicity's grandfather standing at the garden fence. "It is Felicity in her red cloak and Elizabeth in her blue cloak. I thought you two young ladies were a cardinal and a bluebird perched on that garden bench. What a pleasant sight to see!"

"Grandfather!" called Felicity. She and Elizabeth gathered up their dolls and hurried over to him.

"Good day, sir," said Elizabeth. She made a little curtsy.

Grandfather bowed. "Good day, Elizabeth," he said. He nodded at the dolls. "Will you ladies do me the honor of introducing me to your friends?"

The girls looked at each other and giggled. "Oh, Grandfather," said Felicity. "You remember my doll, Susannah Maria Augusta Eliza Lucy Louise."

"Ah, yes, indeed," said Grandfather. "But somehow I can never remember her name. That is, I can't remember *all* of her name."

"My doll's name is Charlotte," said Elizabeth.

"Charlotte!" said Grandfather. "Is she named after Queen Charlotte, the wife of King George, ruler of England and all the colonies?"

"Yes," said Elizabeth.

"Then this is indeed an honor," said Grandfather. "She is loyal to the king, and there aren't many of us Loyalists left. Some are in jail, some have fled to England, and some have changed their minds and become Patriots." He looked at Elizabeth sadly. "Your family and I are among the last Loyalists."

"Aye, sir," said Elizabeth.

"Well!" said Grandfather briskly. "It's too sunny today to talk about cloudy subjects. I've been in Williamsburg for three weeks. It's been rainy and I've had a cold ever since I arrived. This is the first day I've been able to be out of doors. Would you ladies like to come with me while I inspect my horse Penny? I must be sure she is being well cared for."

Grandfather pretended to look stern, which made the girls laugh out loud. Grandfather knew that no horse in Virginia was better cared for than Penny.

"I think you will be pleased with Penny," said Felicity. She led Grandfather and Elizabeth into the stable behind the Merrimans' house. It smelled of horses, leather, and straw. "She's not skittish anymore, and she's stout and healthy." Felicity handed her doll to Elizabeth. Then she backed Penny out of her stall.

Penny stood calmly while Grandfather patted her neck and stroked her sides.

"Stout, indeed!" said Grandfather in a pleased voice. "Penny is going to have a foal this spring."

"Oh!" gasped Felicity and Elizabeth together.

"How wonderful!" said Felicity. "When will the foal be born?"

"I can't be certain," said Grandfather. "But I think Penny will be ready to foal in two or three months."

Felicity stroked Penny's neck and asked, "Will she be all right, Grandfather? Will it harm her to have a foal?"

"Penny is young and strong," said Grandfather. "She should come through the birthing well, as long as there are no unusual problems."

"Oh, Grandfather," said Felicity. "I hope you'll be here in Williamsburg when the foal is born. I won't know what to do when it happens."

"I shall try to be here," said Grandfather. "But your father and Marcus know very well how to help Penny. Indeed, they've known for a long while that Penny is with foal. They wanted me to have the pleasure of telling you." He coughed and cleared his throat. "It is too cold in this stable for my old bones. Shall we go inside now and tell your mother the news about Penny?"

"Aye," said Felicity. She led Penny into her stall and gave her one last hug. Then she followed Grandfather and Elizabeth to the house, smiling to herself. *Penny is going to have a foal!* she thought. *What a wonderful spring this will be!*

Mother, Nan, and William were sitting by the fire in the parlor. Mother held baby Polly in her arms. Polly was a month old. She was a plump, rosy baby with sky-blue eyes and hair as orange as carrots. Nan held the fire screen to protect Polly's face from the heat of the fire, and William was making a jumping jack dance to amuse her. The baby waved her tiny arms and gurgled.

"Mother!" exclaimed Felicity. "Penny is going to have a foal in the spring! Grandfather just told us! Isn't it wonderful?"

"Aye!" agreed Mrs. Merriman. "It's very fine indeed!"

"A foal!" said Nan. "Oh, Lissie, how lovely!"

"May I ride it?" asked William.

"You'll have to wait for the foal to grow, William," said Mother. "Perhaps you can help Felicity care for it."

"Aye," said Grandfather. "Felicity will have to give it a lot of good care."

"Felicity has been a wonderful help taking care of her baby sister," said Mother. "I'm sure she'll do a fine job with Penny's foal, too."

"Oh, I love taking care of Polly!" said Felicity. "And I'll love caring for Penny's foal. I can't wait till it's born! It's such a happy thing to look forward to."

Grandfather took baby Polly from Mother's arms. "Nothing is happier than a new life starting," he said. He kissed the baby's round cheek. "Nothing is sweeter than a baby. Isn't that right, Polly?"

Polly cooed and Mother smiled.

"Mother," said Felicity, "may Elizabeth and I go to the store and tell Ben? He'll be so pleased to hear about Penny's foal."

"You may go," said Mrs. Merriman, "but remember to put on your pattens. The streets are dreadfully muddy from all the rain we've had."

"Yes, Mother," said Felicity. She tickled Polly under her soft chin, and then she and Elizabeth left.

Felicity's pattens lifted her feet above the mud, but it was hard to run or skip while wearing them.

So Felicity and Elizabeth walked as quickly as they could to Mr. Merriman's store. The streets of Williamsburg were crowded these days. Men from all over the colony were coming to Williamsburg to join the army that was forming to fight against the king's soldiers.

Mr. Merriman's store was full of customers. Many of the men wore dark, fringed hunting shirts that were the uniform of Virginia soldiers. The store smelled of spices and soap and wood smoke. Felicity grinned. She loved her father's store, especially when it was full of people and noise and activity, as it was today. Sometimes lately, when the store was very busy, Mr. Merriman let Felicity work there along with Ben and Marcus. She always felt proud and very grown-up when she stood behind the counter. *Maybe I can help out today*, she thought.

Elizabeth tugged at Felicity's sleeve and pointed toward the back of the store. "There's Ben," she said. "He's helping that tall man."

Both girls waved. Ben nodded to them and came over as soon as he was free. "How may I help you ladies today?" he asked.

"We have the most wonderful news!" exclaimed

Felicity. "Penny is going to have a foal this spring!"

"A foal!" said Ben. He smiled. "Good for Penny! Her foal will be the finest in all of Virginia, I'm sure!"

Mr. Merriman joined them with a laugh. "So your grandfather told you the news about Penny!" he said. "I knew you'd be happy, Lissie. No one loves horses more than you do." He turned to Ben and said, "That reminds me, Ben. Have you delivered the curry combs Mr. Pelham ordered for his horses?"

"No, sir," said Ben. "Not yet."

"I know you have been busy," said Mr. Merriman, "but 'tis bad to make Mr. Pelham wait."

"We'll do it!" Felicity offered. "Elizabeth and I can make the delivery for you, Father."

"Very well," said Mr. Merriman. "I might have known that you would volunteer when you heard there were horses involved!" He handed Felicity a bundle wrapped in paper. "Mr. Pelham will pay you. Bring the money back to me." Just then, someone called for Mr. Merriman. "Ben and I had better go back to work," he said. "Thank you for your help, girls!"

# Friends Divided

## CHAPTER 12

**F**elicity and Elizabeth set forth to deliver the curry combs to Mr. Pelham, the town jailer.
He lived in a little house next to the jail, which stood at the edge of Williamsburg.

"Lissie," said Elizabeth, as they walked, "is Mr. Nye still in jail?"

"Yes," said Felicity, "and I am very glad he is. As long as he is in jail, I don't have to worry that he'll come bother Penny."

"He won't be in jail forever," said Elizabeth. "Someday he'll pay the debt he owes and get out of jail."

"I suppose so," said Felicity. She stepped around a puddle.

"Well," Elizabeth asked, "when he does get out of jail, what will you do?"

Felicity shuddered. "Nothing at all," she said firmly.

"I don't want to have *anything* to do with Mr. Nye. He's mean."

"Maybe you could speak to him," said Elizabeth. "Maybe you could make him promise to stay away from Penny and her foal. Maybe—"

"Humph!" snorted Felicity. "You don't know him, Elizabeth. A promise from Mr. Nye isn't worth dust."

Elizabeth said no more. They had reached Mr. Pelham's house. It was connected to the jail, which looked gloomy even in the afternoon sunshine. Felicity knocked on Mr. Pelham's stout wooden door. She and Elizabeth waited on the doorstep for a few minutes. At last, Mr. Pelham opened the door.

"Yes?" he said. "What is it?"

"Good afternoon, sir," said Felicity. "We're delivering your curry combs from Merriman's store." She held out the bundle.

"Ah, yes, indeed," said Mr. Pelham. "Thank you! 'Tis good of you to bring them to my house! Come in for a moment while I find money to pay you."

The two girls stepped inside Mr. Pelham's house as he went on, "I don't have time to get to the store these days. The jail is crowded since they've started arresting

Loyalists. I'm so busy, I just . . ." He stopped and looked around. "Oh bother!" he said. "I've left my money in my coat pocket, and I've left my coat in the passage. If you'll just follow me . . ."

He lit a candle and led the girls to the passage that connected his house to the jail. "Come along this way," he said. "I've got the—"

Suddenly, they all heard a muffled thump, and then someone started coughing violently and choking. Felicity realized she was standing next to the door of a cell. The sounds came from inside.

"Oh dear!" exclaimed Mr. Pelham. "Stay right here, girls! I've got to help." His keys jangled as he hurriedly unlocked the door and rushed into the cell.

Felicity and Elizabeth shivered a little. But they couldn't help peering after him. The cell was small and cold and dark. Mr. Pelham had set his candle on the floor. By its eerie light, the girls saw the jailer easing a man's body back onto a pallet. The body sagged as if it had no bones. The head rolled toward them and Felicity gasped.

The man's eyes were closed. His skin was ghostly white. He was shrunken and thin enough to seem almost transparent. But Felicity was sure that the lifeless lump on the pallet was her old enemy. She swallowed hard and whispered to Elizabeth, "That is Mr. Nye!"

Elizabeth's eyes widened, but she said nothing. Both girls stepped back quickly as Mr. Pelham came out of the cell and locked the door behind him.

"That's Mr. Nye, isn't it?" Felicity asked.

"Aye," said Mr. Pelham.

"Is he . . . is he dead?" Elizabeth whispered.

"Near to it," said Mr. Pelham. "He's had the fever for days. He's got no money to buy logs for a fire, or a blanket, or medicine." The jailer shook his head. "Jiggy Nye used to be a respected man. No one in Williamsburg knew more about animals. But after his wife died, he took to drinking. He drank in hate with every drop. He's been in the stocks and pillory many times. Now he's ended up here, in debtors' jail, with no one to care if he lives or dies."

After Mr. Pelham paid for the curry combs, Felicity and Elizabeth said good-bye. The sky was a wintry pink as they walked away from the jail. Felicity felt cold. She pulled her cloak close around her. But the chill she felt was inside and would not go away.

Felicity and Elizabeth walked together silently through the January dusk. Mr. Nye's face haunted Felicity. She could not forget how helpless and sad he looked. Then Felicity shook herself. *Mr. Nye might be sick,* she thought, *but he is still the man who treated Penny so badly. I will not feel sorry for him . . .*

Elizabeth looked over at Felicity. "It was terrible in that cell, wasn't it?" she said. "It was so dark and so cold. No one should have to live in a place like that, especially someone who is sick, with no one to care for him."

Felicity said firmly, "It is Mr. Nye's own fault he has no friends. He is cold-hearted and cruel."

"He looked like a weak, helpless old man to me," said Elizabeth softly.

"Maybe so, but you don't know him!" said Felicity.

"That is true," said Elizabeth. She faced Felicity. "Don't you feel sorry for him at all?" she asked.

"Well," said Felicity. "He did look miserable. But after the way he treated Penny, I could never feel sorry for him."

"I think we should bring him a blanket and some

medicine," said Elizabeth. She sounded gentle but determined. "I think we should help him."

"No!" said Felicity. "Not Mr. Nye! He would never accept anything from me anyway. He hates me as much as I hate him."

"He doesn't need to know it's from you," said Elizabeth. "No one needs to know."

"Elizabeth," said Felicity, "even if I did feel sorry for him, a little bit, why should I be kind to him? Why should I help him? If he does get better, he may come looking for Penny."

"Then that's when you tell him you were the one who helped him," said Elizabeth. "He won't hate you if you've been kind to him. He won't hurt Penny."

"It won't do any good," said Felicity. "Mr. Nye will never change."

"Aye, you are right," said Elizabeth. "He won't change if you do nothing. But if you help him, there is a chance he *will* change."

"You don't understand," said Felicity. "Mr. Nye said he would kill Penny before he'd let me have her. He meant it, too."

"He may have meant it when he said it," replied

Elizabeth. "But if you do something nice for him, he won't want to hurt you or your horse. Don't you see, Felicity? If you help him, you will be doing something to protect Penny and her foal."

Felicity thought about what Elizabeth had said. After a long while she turned and said, "Very well. I'll do it. But only because of Penny."

"Good!" said Elizabeth.

"I have an old horse blanket we can give him," said Felicity, "and Mother and I made garlic syrup for Grandfather's cold. I'll mix up more."

"I can bring a blanket, too," said Elizabeth. "I'll come to your house tomorrow at three o'clock. Then we'll go to the jail."

"Tomorrow at three," repeated Felicity as the girls parted to go to their homes.

───❧✿❧───

But Elizabeth did not come to Felicity's house the next day at three o'clock. Felicity was puzzled. She waited almost an hour, and then she went to Elizabeth's house to find her.

Felicity was carrying a basket with the old horse

blanket and a bottle of medicine in it. She had pinned a note to the blanket that said, *For Jiggy Nye.* The basket was heavy. It banged against Felicity's knees with every step.

Felicity knocked on the door of the Coles' house for a long time before a servant answered. He opened the door just a bit and stuck his head out. "I'm very sorry, miss," he said. He sounded flustered. "Mrs. Cole and her daughters are not receiving callers." He started to close the door.

"Wait!" Felicity exclaimed. "You know me. I'm Felicity Merriman, Elizabeth's friend. Whatever is the matter? Why can't I see Elizabeth?"

"I beg your pardon, Miss Felicity," the servant said. "You can't come in. I'm sorry. You'll have to go." He closed the door quite firmly.

Felicity was confused and worried. *Something awful must have happened!* she thought. *Someone must be terribly sick. I wonder if it's Elizabeth!* Felicity knocked on the door again, but no one came. She looked up at the window of Elizabeth's room, but she couldn't see anything. She walked around to the back of the house. Everything was shut tight, as if the Coles had gone away.

Felicity gave up. She walked to the jail without thinking about where she was going. She had just put the basket next to the doorstep of Mr. Pelham's house when the door opened. Quickly, she stood in front of the basket to hide it.

"Oh, it's you again," said Mr. Pelham. "Why are you back?"

"I . . . I think I left something here," said Felicity.

"Well, I haven't time to help look for it," said Mr. Pelham impatiently. "I'm busy. They've just brought another Loyalist here. I don't know how I'm supposed to find room for him. The jail's over-crowded as it is without this new one, this fine and fancy gentleman, Mr. Cole."

*Mr. Cole?* Elizabeth's father? Felicity was stunned. "It can't be Mr. Cole," she said to the jailer. "Why would Mr. Cole be put in jail?"

"He's a Loyalist," shrugged Mr. Pelham. "That's reason enough."

"But that's not fair!" Felicity exclaimed. "Mr. Cole hasn't done anything wrong! You can't—"

"Now, miss!" interrupted Mr. Pelham. "I didn't arrest him! And I can't stand here arguing with you.

You'll have to go." He closed the door.

Felicity turned away. She could not believe what she'd heard. Elizabeth's father was in jail! He was locked away in a cold, dark cell just like a horse thief. And all because he was a Loyalist. *No wonder I wasn't allowed into the Coles' house today,* she thought. *They know Father is a Patriot. They probably don't trust anyone in the colony today.*

Felicity knew there had been battles between the king's soldiers and the Patriots' army in Massachusetts and Canada and nearby Norfolk. She had seen soldiers with their guns, training to fight, right on Market Square in Williamsburg. But none of that had affected anyone she loved. Now it seemed that what she had feared most was happening. The fight between the Patriots and the Loyalists was changing everything. It was going to separate her from her friend.

Suddenly Felicity wanted to see her own father. She wanted to be sure he was safe, and to feel safe herself. She ran to Father's store.

Father, Grandfather, and Ben were talking in Father's office. It was warm there, and gently lit by candles. Father smiled as Felicity came in. "Your grandfather and I can't agree about when Penny's foal is going to be born," he said. "I think it will be sooner than . . ." He stopped when he saw Felicity's face in the light. "Why, Lissie!" he said. "What's the matter?"

"Patriots put Mr. Cole in jail," said Felicity, "just because he is a Loyalist."

"Elizabeth's father?" gasped Ben. "In jail?"

"Aye!" said Felicity. "In a cold, dark cell, just like Mr. Nye!"

"This is an outrage!" exclaimed Grandfather. He was furious. "This just cannot be possible!"

"I'm afraid anything is possible these days," said Mr. Merriman.

"The Coles' servant wouldn't even allow me to talk to Elizabeth," said Felicity. "Does Mrs. Cole think I'm an enemy because you're a Patriot, Father?"

Father put his arm around Felicity's shoulders. "Elizabeth knows you are her friend," he said. "Never fear."

Ben tried to comfort her, too. "The day after next is Sunday," he said. "You'll see Elizabeth at church. You'll be able to speak to her there."

Felicity hoped he was right.

# Grandfather's Errand

## CHAPTER 13

**S**unday morning was gray and bitterly cold. Felicity kept her hands in her mitts and muff as the family walked to church. She held tightly to something special she'd tucked inside her muff to give Elizabeth if she had the chance. She looked for Elizabeth in the churchyard but did not see her.

The service had just begun when a whisper swept through the church. Felicity looked around to see Mrs. Cole leading Elizabeth and Annabelle down the aisle. Mrs. Cole held her head high. Elizabeth's face was hidden by the hood of her blue cloak. Felicity could not catch her eye.

After the service, the Coles left the church quickly. Felicity hurried after them. "Elizabeth!" she called. "Wait!"

Elizabeth turned around, but Mrs. Cole took her

firmly by the hand and pulled her away. Felicity ran to catch up. "Elizabeth!" she said. "Take this!" From her muff she pulled the sampler of stitches she had finished last spring. There was a bluebird on it, just the color of Elizabeth's cloak. And under the bluebird it said: *Faithful Friends Forever Be.* Felicity thrust the sampler into Elizabeth's hand.

Elizabeth looked at it and gave Felicity a sad smile before her mother hurried her away.

Felicity felt Grandfather's hand on her shoulder. Together, they watched Elizabeth disappear. "I hate to see Elizabeth so unhappy," said Felicity. "I wish I could break open the jail! I wish I could smash the door down and help Mr. Cole escape! I want to do something, *anything*, to help."

"I'm sure you do," said Grandfather. "I do, too."

Icy rain fell all that day, all night long, and on into the morning. The next day the ground was slick and the trees groaned under a coating of ice. Mrs. Merriman would not allow the children to go out of doors. They played together in front of the parlor fire. Felicity sat on the floor with baby Polly in her lap. It was comforting to hold Polly's warm little body, and spin the top for her, and listen to her coo with delight.

"Felicity," asked Mother, "have you seen Grandfather this morning?"

"No, Mother," said Felicity. "Not since breakfast."

"Oh, dear," fretted Mrs. Merriman. "He's gone out in this weather! It will make his cold worse!" She looked out the window at the freezing rain. "Why didn't he wait until the rain stopped? What urgent errand could he have had?"

Felicity could see that her mother was very worried. "I don't know, Mother," she said. "Grandfather didn't say anything to me."

Mrs. Merriman grew more and more worried as she waited for Grandfather to return. It was almost dinnertime before they heard him come in the door. Mrs. Merriman ran to greet him. "Where have you been?" she fussed. "You're soaked to the skin! I'll take your cloak. Go and sit by the fire."

Grandfather sank into the chair by the fire. His face was pale. He sounded tired when he said, "Felicity, come here."

Felicity put Polly in her cradle and went over to stand next to Grandfather's chair. "Yes, Grandfather?"

Grandfather coughed and cleared his throat. "My business today had to do with you," he said, "and your friend Elizabeth and her family. I went to see her father today."

"You went to the jail?" asked Felicity.

"Yes," said Grandfather. He shivered. "What a dismal, dreadful place it is! I spoke to Mr. Cole. He is a fine gentleman. After our conversation, I went to the authorities."

Mother gasped. Grandfather went on to say, "Now that the king's royal governor is gone, Williamsburg is governed by the Committee of Safety. The chairman of the Committee is Edmund Pendleton."

Grandfather paused for breath. His eyes had a bit of their old twinkle in them. "Well!" he said. "I've known Pendleton since he was a young pup! I went straight to him, and I said, 'Stop this nonsense, Pendleton! Release Mr. Cole. I have his word as a gentleman that he has not caused any trouble. And if you need another Loyalist to fill Mr. Cole's place in jail, take me!'"

Grandfather laughed so hard he made himself cough. When he could speak again, he said, "I wish you could have seen Pendleton's face. It was as purple as a turnip! He mumbled and chattered about how being a Loyalist was treasonous to Virginia. He said he would have to present the matter to the Committee of Safety and then speak to Mr. Cole himself. He blustered and fussed, but in the end he had to admit that Mr. Cole had done nothing wrong, so he would try to have him released."

"Does that mean Mr. Cole will go home?" asked William.

"Yes," said Grandfather. "I believe he will go home."

"Hurray!" shouted Nan and William.

"Oh, Grandfather!" exclaimed Felicity. "Thank you! Elizabeth will be so happy!" She kissed his cheek. "I'm happy, too."

Mother's eyes were full of love as she looked at Grandfather. "It's a fine thing you've done this morning," she said. "I hope it hasn't been too much for you."

"I do feel a bit feverish," admitted Grandfather. "I'd like to rest now. Don't worry about my dinner. I'm more tired than hungry."

Felicity helped him out of his chair. He leaned on her as he went slowly up the stairs to his chamber. He

seemed worn-out and frail. But as Felicity was closing
his door behind her, she heard him chuckle and say to
himself, "Pendleton, hah! Purple as a turnip he was!"
She smiled and skipped down the stairs. Grandfather
had set everything right.

After dinner, Felicity asked her mother, "May I go
see Elizabeth now?"

"No, I don't think you should," said Mother. "This
has been very hard on Mrs. Cole. It may take some time
for her to feel friendly toward any family that supports
the Patriots. We must wait and see how she feels about
your friendship with Elizabeth. You had better wait
for Mrs. Cole to allow Elizabeth to come to you. Be
patient."

Felicity was disappointed. She was aching to see her
friend. She decided to go to Father's store. Its cheery
bustle always made her happy, and she wanted to tell
Father what Grandfather had done for Mr. Cole.

Felicity took the long way around to the store so
that she could walk past Elizabeth's house. She stopped in front. Sleet stung her eyes as she looked up at

Elizabeth's window. She couldn't see any movement inside, just something propped on the windowsill. Felicity squinted to see better. It was a needlework frame holding the sampler Felicity had given to Elizabeth. Felicity wanted to dance for happiness. She knew Elizabeth meant the message for her: *Faithful Friends Forever Be.*

The next day, a pale winter sun shone, but it wasn't warm enough to melt the brittle ice coating the trees. Felicity was up early. As she led Penny from her stall to exercise her, Ben came down from his room above the stable.

"Good morning!" he said. "How is Penny today?"

"She's fine," said Felicity. "Father says I shouldn't ride her. He thinks her foal will be born quite soon."

Ben followed along as Felicity walked Penny around the stable yard.

"Well," he said with a grin. "I don't know much about foals, but Penny is so big, I'd say your father is right."

"I'm glad you'll be here when it's born," said

Felicity. "If you had run away to be a soldier in General Washington's army, you'd never have known about Penny's foal."

Ben looked serious. "I promised your father I'd stay at the store until I'm eighteen," he said. "I won't break my promise. But when that day comes, I'll go fight with the Patriots. I won't change my mind about that. Not ever."

Felicity sighed. "You're just as stubborn as Grandfather," she said. "He'll never change his mind about the king. He'll always be a Loyalist."

"Your grandfather and I will never agree," Ben said. He and Felicity led Penny back to the stable and into her stall. "But I do respect him."

"I do, too!" agreed Felicity. "I'm so happy that he helped Mr. Cole. Grandfather made everything all right again, just as it was before."

"No, Lissie," said Ben sadly. "Not even your grandfather could do that."

But Felicity ran ahead of Ben to the house, so she did not hear him.

"Where's Grandfather?" she asked, as she sat at the breakfast table.

"The fever is much worse," said Mother, "and 'tis hard for him to breathe. Rose has mixed some molasses, vinegar, and butter for him to drink to ease the pain in his throat. Father and Mr. Galt, the apothecary, are with him now."

Ben, Felicity, Nan, and William looked at each other. They knew by the way Mother spoke that Grandfather was very ill. After breakfast, Ben left for the store. The children went into the parlor. They played quietly with Polly.

Soon after Father and the apothecary left, Mother came into the parlor. Felicity could tell she had been crying. "Felicity," Mother said, "Grandfather is asking for you."

Felicity hurried up the stairs and tiptoed into Grandfather's shadowy chamber. Grandfather was lying very still. His breathing was slow and his skin was ashy gray. Felicity stood next to him and took his hand. Grandfather opened his eyes.

"Don't try to talk, Grandfather," said Felicity softly. "You just lie there. I'll read to you."

Grandfather closed his eyes again.

"'The Lord is my shepherd,'" Felicity read from the

Bible, "'therefore I lack nothing. He shall feed me in a green pasture; and lead me forth beside the waters of comfort . . .'"

Felicity looked at Grandfather and smiled. "That part always makes me think of your plantation," she said. "I imagine lying in the green grass in the big pasture on the hill on a sunny day. And the river is comforting. It's peaceful, the way it flows along so smoothly. You'll be back there soon, Grandfather. You'll feel fine once you get back to your plantation."

Grandfather reached up and stroked her cheek. "Dear Lissie," he whispered. He sighed and went to sleep. Felicity kissed his forehead and then tiptoed away.

Days passed, and Grandfather grew weaker and weaker. One night, after Felicity and Nan went to bed in the chamber they were sharing while Grandfather visited, Felicity heard voices and saw light moving in the passage outside their door. *Has the apothecary come back again?* she wondered. Nan woke up, too. They lay in the dark, listening.

In a little while, the door opened and Mother came in. She put the candlestick on the table, sat on the bed, and took each of them by the hand.

"My dear girls," she said in a shaky voice. "Your grandfather died . . . just a few minutes ago." Her voice faltered, and then she said softly, "He loved you both very, very much. God rest his soul."

Nan cried bitterly. Felicity was silent as she clung to her mother. Her sorrow was too great to be eased by crying. Mother sat with Nan and Felicity until the sky lightened to gray and the last star disappeared.

# Into the Valley

randfather's burial was to take place at his plantation on the York River. Mother and the children rode together in a carriage. Father rode on horseback. Marcus drove the cart that carried Grandfather's coffin. The roads were muddy and so deeply rutted that the carriage jolted and swayed. Felicity hardly noticed. She felt numb, as if all the life in her had died, too.

As they rode up the drive to Grandfather's plantation, Felicity looked out at the dreary landscape. When she had last seen the plantation, at the end of the summer, it was alive with color. Now the pastures were brown, the trees inky black, and the river a cold, dull silver. Her first view of the river used to make Felicity's spirits soar. Today she felt no joy.

Grandfather was buried on a windy bluff above the

river. Felicity set her jaw and would not allow herself to cry as she listened to the minister read the end of the psalm she had read to Grandfather. "Yea, though I walk through the valley of the shadow of death, I will fear no evil . . ."

The words did not comfort her. Felicity was angry at the world and angry at the God who had taken her grandfather away from her. She was fearful, too. Nothing seemed safe anymore. How could she trust a world where such sorrowful things as death happened? How could she feel safe when Grandfather was not there to protect her, understand her, and love her? She was glad the blustery wind blew the minister's words away.

After supper, the children were sent to bed. Felicity wasn't sleepy. She sat by the window watching the gray sky turn black.

"Felicity," she heard Mother say. When Felicity turned, she saw Mother standing behind her, holding a small trunk. "This was in Grandfather's chamber. He meant to give it to you on your birthday. I think you should have it now."

She put the trunk on the floor, and Felicity knelt to

open it. She lifted out a riding habit made of deep green wool, the color of forest pines. At the sight of it, all the tears Felicity had been holding back burst forth. *Oh, Grandfather,* Felicity thought. *You and I will never ride together again. I will never be able to thank you for this, or laugh with you, or hug you ever again.* Felicity buried her face in her arms and sobbed.

Mother knelt beside her and put her arms around Felicity. "It makes me so sad," gasped Felicity, "when I think of riding with Grandfather . . ."

"Aye," said Mother. "Memories can make your heart ache with sorrow. But it is good to remember happy times with your Grandfather. Indeed, as long as you remember him, he won't be truly gone from you."

"But he *is* gone," said Felicity passionately. "Oh, I wish I could go back. I want to go back to last summer, when Grandfather was well and we were all so happy together!"

"I understand," said Mother. She looked out the window. "This plantation is where I grew up," she said. "Sometimes when I am here, I ask myself, would I go back and be a child, be with my mother and father again, if I could? Those were lovely days." She paused, and then said, "But then I think . . . ah, how could I live without my sweet Lissie, and Nan, and William, and Polly? How could I be happy without my dear husband? No, as much as I miss my mother and now my father, I wouldn't go back, even if I could. That's as it should be. We're meant to grow and learn and change."

"No!" said Felicity. "I hate changes!"

"Not all changes are bad," said Mrs. Merriman. "Think of how you've changed in the past year. You're not the flighty, headstrong child you used to be. You're steady and thoughtful, even if you are still sometimes impatient. And think of all the happy changes you have to look forward to. You'll see Elizabeth again. You'll see Polly learn to walk and talk and become a little person. You'll see Penny's foal be born and grow up." She brushed the tears from Felicity's cheek. "Face those changes with faith and hope, my child, not fear."

"How can I hope for anything, when Grandfather is dead?" asked Felicity. "Death is the end of everything."

"No," said Mother, holding Felicity tightly. "No change, no loss, no separation, not even death, can end love." She kissed Felicity's flushed forehead and left.

Felicity cried until she felt hollow. After a long while, she fell asleep.

Mother and the children went home a few days after Grandfather's burial. As the carriage lurched along the road to Williamsburg, William asked, "Mother, why isn't Father coming home, too?"

"Your father and Marcus stayed at the plantation to put Grandfather's business affairs in order," said Mother. "They'll be home soon."

William looked as if he might cry. "But I don't want Father gone," he said. "I want him to be home with us."

Felicity felt sorry for William. *He's probably afraid Father will go away forever, like Grandfather,* she thought. "Don't worry, William," she said. "Father will be home before you know it. And meanwhile, Mother and I will look after you, and you and Nan must help us look after baby Polly."

William brightened, and Mother smiled at Felicity gratefully.

Ben was at the front door of the house to greet them as the carriage pulled up. He helped Mrs. Merriman step down. "Thank you, Ben," she said. "Mr. Merriman and Marcus will be gone for a few weeks. Will you be able to take care of the store in their absence?"

"Yes, ma'am," said Ben.

"Good lad," said Mrs. Merriman. She turned to Felicity. "I am sure Ben could use an extra pair of hands today, Lissie," she said. "Would you like to help him in the store?"

"Yes," said Felicity. "Yes, I would."

"Off you go then," said Mother. She knew that no place was more likely to cheer Felicity than her father's store.

And indeed, the store was so bustling all afternoon, Felicity was too busy to be sad. She and Ben walked home together in the twilight after they closed the store. "Thank you for your help," said Ben. "You know just what to do in the store. You were a good apprentice today."

Felicity just nodded.

Ben looked at her. "Lissie," he said, "I know you are very sad about your grandfather. I'm sorry, too. He was a fine old gentleman. No one can replace him." They walked on, and then Ben said, "You helped me when

I was hurt and . . . and unhappy this summer. I wish I could help you now."

Felicity smiled for the first time in a long time. "Thank you, Ben," she said. "You are a kind friend."

Over the next few days, the air seemed to soften. It sometimes carried hints that spring was coming. Sorrow still overcame Felicity whenever she thought about Grandfather. There were reminders of him everywhere. Whenever she heard music, or when she played the guitar he had given her, Felicity thought of her grandfather's gravelly voice singing along, happily out of tune. Whenever she cared for Penny, she remembered the day Grandfather had told her she could bring Penny back to Williamsburg with her. Whenever she held Polly, she thought of how Grandfather had said, *Nothing is happier than a new life starting. Nothing is sweeter than a baby.*

She was thinking of Grandfather one afternoon as she worked in her garden, pulling away dead leaves to prepare the ground for spring planting, just as he had taught her. Felicity looked up and saw Elizabeth running toward her, her familiar blue cloak flying behind her as she ran.

"Felicity!" gasped Elizabeth, all out of breath. "Oh, I am so glad to see you!"

Felicity hugged her friend. "I am glad to see you, too!" she said.

Elizabeth's eyes filled with tears. "When I heard that your grandfather died, my heart ached for you," she said. "And Mother felt so sorry. She never thanked him for getting Father released from jail."

"You must be happy to have your father home now," said Felicity.

"Aye," said Elizabeth. "He will be home for a while. But he had to promise to leave the colony. He's going to New York. It's safer for Loyalists there."

"New York!" exclaimed Felicity. "Oh, no! Elizabeth! You are not going to leave, too, are you?"

"No," said Elizabeth. "Mother and Annabelle and I will stay here to look after our property."

"Ah," said Felicity. "You will miss your father most terribly, won't you?"

"I will," said Elizabeth. "But at least I know he'll be safe, and not in that awful jail." She sighed. "Mother and Annabelle and I will have to take care of ourselves. Things are different now. Many things have changed."

"Aye," said Felicity sadly. "Everything has changed."

"I know one thing that has not changed," said Elizabeth. "You are still my best friend."

The girls smiled at each other.

"I thought about you every day," said Elizabeth. "I wondered what you were doing. Did you ever go to the jail?"

"Yes," said Felicity. "I left a blanket and some medicine by the door."

"I wonder if Mr. Nye got them," said Elizabeth. "I wonder if he's better now, or if he . . ."

Felicity had been wondering the very same things. "Perhaps we could go to the jail," she said. "Perhaps we could ask Mr. Pelham about Mr. Nye."

"Yes!" said Elizabeth. "Let's go now!"

Mr. Pelham's smile was wide when he saw the girls at the door of his house. "Good day, young ladies!" he said. "What are you delivering today?"

"Mr. Pelham," said Felicity, "we came to ask about someone. We were wondering . . . how is Mr. Nye?"

"He's not here!" said Mr. Pelham happily. "He paid his debt. He's gone."

"But he was so ill," said Felicity, "and he had no money, or friends . . ."

"Bless my soul!" said Mr. Pelham. "It turned out that Jiggy Nye *did* have friends. Soon after you two young ladies came to deliver the curry combs, the most curious thing happened. I found a basket outside this very door with a blanket and some medicine in it for Jiggy Nye. I never did see who left it." He looked at Felicity and Elizabeth. "Was it the two of you together?"

"No," said Elizabeth in her sweet voice. "It was not the two of us together."

Mr. Pelham went on, "Well, then the most curious thing of all happened a few days later! Along came an old gentleman. His health was poor but his spirit was strong. He came to the jail to see that other gentleman, the Loyalist, Mr. Cole. After he spoke to Mr. Cole, he asked to see Jiggy Nye."

Felicity and Elizabeth looked at each other in amazement. They knew Mr. Pelham was talking about Grandfather.

"I told the old gentleman that Mr. Nye was too ill to talk," said Mr. Pelham. "He left me money and told me to tell Jiggy Nye that he owed him the money for a horse. He said something about a penny, but he left me a great deal more money than that! When Mr. Nye was better, I gave him the money. He understood the old gentleman's message even if I didn't. Mr. Nye used the money to pay off most of his debt. He's working for me, caring for my horses, to pay off the rest of it. He's a good man with animals when he's not drinking. And I think from now on he'll stay away from the bottle."

Mr. Pelham smiled again. "That blanket and medicine did more than help cure Jiggy Nye of his illness. It seemed to cure him of his meanness, too. I always thought there was still some goodness left in old Jiggy Nye. And I was right. It just needed the kindness of friends to bring it out."

Felicity's heart was too full for her to speak. Grandfather had given Mr. Nye money for Penny. Grandfather *had* fixed everything. Thanks to his kindness, she needn't fear Mr. Nye or what he might do to Penny or her foal. *Thank you, Grandfather,* she thought. *Oh, thank you!*

# Patriot

elicity! Wake up!"

Felicity woke from a deep sleep to see Mother and Ben standing next to her bed. "What is it?" she asked. "What's the matter?"

"It's Penny," said Ben. "I think she's going to have her foal."

"Oh, no!" said Felicity. She jumped out of bed and pulled on stockings and shoes as Mother wrapped a cloak around her. "Father is gone and so is Marcus! What shall we do?"

"There's no need to fret," said Mother, as they all hurried out to the stable. "Penny will be fine."

Ben lit a lantern and hung it on a nail in Penny's stall. Penny was lying on the straw. Her sides were heaving.

Felicity knelt down and stroked Penny's neck.

"Penny! Penny, my girl," murmured Felicity. "Oh, Penny! Are you all right?"

Ben looked worried. "The foal is having trouble," he said. "Something is not right. I don't know what to do. We need to get help."

Felicity stood up. "Mother, you hold Penny's head and try to keep her quiet," she said. "I'll go get help."

"Take the lantern!" called Mother.

But Felicity did not need the lantern, though the night was starless. She knew the way through the garden, through the dark streets, past the sleeping houses, to the edge of town. She had run this way many, many times on those cool mornings before dawn when she had sneaked off to see Penny in the pasture. She knew exactly where she was going—to find Mr. Nye.

Mr. Nye's house was a tumble-down shack next to the tannery. It looked ghostly and forbidding, blacker than the night around it. Felicity pounded on the door.

"Mr. Nye! Mr. Nye!" she cried. "Please! Please help me!"

The door opened and Mr. Nye stood there, holding a candle that cast light on his craggy face. "You!" he said, when he saw Felicity.

"You've got to help us, Mr. Nye," said Felicity. "Penny's having her foal. Something's wrong. Mr. Pelham, the jailer, said you know all about animals. Please, will you come help?"

Mr. Nye stared at Felicity. "It was you, wasn't it, who brought that blanket and the medicine to me?" he said in his gruff voice. "And it was your grandfather who left money for me. Don't say it wasn't. I know it was. I owe you a kindness. I'll come with you now."

"Please, make haste!" said Felicity. "We've no time to spare."

Never in her wildest dreams could Felicity have imagined she would be running through the night with Mr. Nye, very glad that he was by her side. But she was. Together, they ran to the Merrimans' stable and hurried inside. When Mr. Nye came into the lantern light and Mother and Ben saw him, they looked horrified.

"What are *you* doing here?" Ben said. "Get away! If you hurt Felicity or Penny, I'll kill you. Mark me, I will!"

"It's all right, Ben," explained Felicity. "I brought him here. He knows how to help Penny."

Ben looked confused. "It's all right, Ben," Felicity said again. "He is a friend."

Mr. Nye turned to Felicity. "You'll have to keep your horse calm," he said. "If she moves suddenly when she sees me, it'll hurt her and the foal. And I don't reckon she's forgotten or forgiven me for the way I treated her."

"I'll keep her calm," said Felicity. She and her mother knelt by Penny's head. They stroked her and murmured soothing words.

Mr. Nye did not make a sound. All his movements were sure. His touch on Penny was gentle. In a short time, the foal was born.

Felicity looked at the beautiful little colt lying on the straw next to Penny. He was black and shiny, with spindly legs. *Grandfather was right*, she thought. *Nothing is happier than a new life starting.* "Oh, Penny," she whispered. "Your colt is perfect." She hugged Penny, and then she hugged Mother. When she looked up to thank Mr. Nye for his help, he was gone.

Ben grinned at the colt. "He's a gawky little thing, isn't he? But he'll grow into those legs," he said. "He'll be a beauty, just like his mother."

"And just as spirited, too," said Mrs. Merriman.

"Aye," said Felicity. "I am sure this colt will be full of independence, just like Penny."

Ben nodded and laughed. "And as full of fire as a Patriot soldier."

"That's what we'll call him," said Felicity. "Patriot."

"Patriot," repeated Mother. "That is a fine, proud name."

By the time Father and Marcus came home, Patriot could already trot around the stable yard on his long, thin legs. "That's the most handsome colt I've ever seen," said Father as he inspected Patriot. "Felicity, you amaze me. There's not another girl in Virginia who could handle the birth of a foal so well."

"Oh, I did nothing, Father!" said Felicity. She swung herself up onto Penny's back. She and Father were going for a ride. It was Penny's first outing since Patriot had been born. "It was Mr. Nye who helped Penny."

"Jiggy Nye?" said Father. "That scoundrel? You went to him for help?"

"Aye," said Felicity. "He is a friend now."

"That is a change," said Father. He was riding Old Bess.

"It was Elizabeth's idea to help him," said Felicity. "He and I wouldn't have become friends if it were not for her and Grandfather."

Mr. Merriman smiled at Felicity. "You and Elizabeth are fine young ladies," he said. "I am proud of you. Your grandfather would be proud, too."

Mr. Merriman and Felicity rode side by side along the street in the cool spring sunshine. Felicity sat tall on Penny's back. She was wearing the dark green riding habit from Grandfather. Whenever she wore it, she thought of Grandfather, and how much she loved him, and how much she missed him. Her memories still made her sad, but it was a gentle sadness, not sharp and bitter anymore.

"I miss Grandfather every day," Felicity said to her father.

"Aye," said Father. "He loved you very much." He looked at Felicity seriously. "Your grandfather left his plantation to Mother and you children," he said. "He knew how much you loved it."

"Does that mean we will live on the plantation now?" asked Felicity.

"Is that what you would like to do?" asked Father.

Felicity took a deep breath. She thought of how lovely the plantation was in the summer. The green fields stretched from the river to the forest, and the air was sweet with the scents of fruits and flowers. Life there flowed along as smoothly as the river. Then she looked around her at the busy streets of Williamsburg, full of people and color, noise and life. She thought of Father's store, and Ben, and Elizabeth.

"No, Father," she said. "I'd rather stay here in Williamsburg."

Father nodded at Felicity. "I'm glad you want to stay," he said. "I fear there are hard times ahead. This will be a long war."

"Father," said Felicity as they rode along, "doesn't the king's army have a lot more soldiers than the Patriots' army?"

"Aye," said Father. "But the war for independence isn't only between armies. The king's army will have to defeat more than soldiers. They'll have to defeat the people themselves, you and me, and everyone like us.

And as long as our hearts and minds are set on independence, as long as we don't give up, no army can defeat us. The war will touch us all. It will be won or lost by us all."

"Will you be a soldier, Father?" asked Felicity.

"No," said Father. "I don't want to fight with a gun. I'm going to help the Patriots in another way. I'm going to be a commissary agent. Marcus and I will travel and collect supplies for the Patriots' army. I will be gone a great deal of the time. I'm relying on you to help Mother with the house and the other children. She says you are a wonderful help to her. And you will have to help Ben, too, in the store. You will not have much time for playing."

"Oh! I love working in the store, Father," said Felicity. "You know I always have! And perhaps by helping you, I will be helping the Patriots, too."

"You will indeed," said Father.

"There is another way I can help," said Felicity. She leaned down and stroked Penny's neck. Then she said slowly, "I can give you Penny. You can ride her when you collect supplies."

"Lissie," said Father. "I know you love Penny very

much. Wouldn't it be hard for you to be separated from her?"

"Aye," said Felicity softly. "But I will be happy knowing that you and Penny are together, looking after each other. I will trust each of you to bring the other back to me safely."

"You are a fine young lady indeed, Lissie!" said Father. They had reached the pastures at the edge of town. "Come along now! Let's take our horses for a trot!"

It was warm the day Father and Marcus set forth on their first trip to collect supplies for the Patriots. Felicity and Ben stood in the doorway of the store, waving good-bye. Felicity felt proud. Father looked handsome and strong, and Penny's coat shone bright as gold in the sunshine. *Good-bye,* she thought as Penny and Father and Marcus disappeared down the dusty, crowded street. *Come back safely, all of you.*

When she could not see them anymore, Felicity turned and followed Ben into the store. She stood as tall as she could behind the counter. Very soon the door opened, and her first customer came in.

"Good day, Miss Merriman!" the customer said. It was Elizabeth.

"Good day, Miss Cole," Felicity said with a smile. "And how may I help you today?"

# INSIDE Felicity's World

The Revolutionary War not only changed the thirteen English colonies into the United States of America—it also changed the city of Williamsburg and the daily lives of families like Felicity's. Before the war, Williamsburg was a bustling center of politics, business, and fashion. It was the capital of Virginia and the most important city in the large colony. But when the Patriots began the fight for independence from England, life in Williamsburg became very different.

Soldiers took over parts of Williamsburg, and soon more than two thousand men were camping out there. Loyalist families, like Elizabeth's, were often separated. Loyalist men could be arrested for supporting the king, just as Mr. Cole was. As a result, many men went back to England or to places like New York City that had been captured by the English. Their wives and children stayed in Williamsburg to protect their homes and property from colonists who were angry at them for being loyal to the king.

Patriot families like Felicity's also were often separated when husbands and older brothers went off to fight. After they left, women and children continued to tend their animals and work in their gardens, and now they had to manage their families' households and businesses, too. There was also more work because many male slaves left to join the army, hoping to gain their freedom.

People in Williamsburg could not buy all the things they could before the war. Shopkeepers had once sold many *imported* goods—goods brought in from England and other countries. But during the war, England stopped selling to the former colonies. And England tried to keep ships from other countries from entering American ports. So people had a hard time finding imported goods such as chocolate, coffee, tea, china, and silk. As the war went on, people made many of the things they needed.

Families worried about the health and safety of their loved ones in the army. Mail was not delivered on a regular schedule during the war, so a letter from a soldier might take months to reach his family. People in Williamsburg and other communities shared whatever information they had about the war. Taverns, where visitors from out of town stayed, buzzed with news about the war.

Soldiers worried about the safety of their families at home as well. In 1780, the capital of Virginia was moved from Williamsburg to Richmond, partly because people worried that Williamsburg might be attacked. A year later, fighting actually took place just outside Williamsburg, and residents like Felicity feared for their lives. Many American families lived near other battlegrounds and felt the same danger.

The fight for independence from England changed the lives of all Americans. Nearly everyone suffered in some way, but they looked forward to being together again when the war was over, as citizens of a new nation—the United States of America.

# Read more of FELICITY'S stories,

available from booksellers and at *americangirl.com*

## ❧ *Classics* ❧

*Felicity's classic series, now in two volumes:*

*Volume 1:*
**Love and Loyalty**
When Felicity falls in love with a beautiful horse, she takes a great risk to save the mare from her cruel owner.

*Volume 2:*
**A Stand for Independence**
Felicity's friend Ben has run off to join the army. Now he needs her help—in secret. Should Felicity break Ben's trust?

## ❧ *Journey in Time* ❧

*Travel back in time—and spend a day with Felicity!*

### Gunpowder and Tea Cakes

Experience the American Revolution with Felicity! Ride horses, visit the Governor's Palace—or get involved in a gunpowder plot! Choose your own path through this multiple-ending story.

## ❧ *Mysteries* ❧

*More thrilling adventures with Felicity!*

### Peril at King's Creek

Felicity is having a wonderful summer at her grandfather's plantation, until she discovers the farm—and her horse—are in danger!

### Traitor in Williamsburg

Father has been accused of being a traitor! When he is arrested, Felicity must find out who is behind the terrible accusation.

### Lady Margaret's Ghost

Felicity doesn't believe in ghosts . . . until odd and eerie things begin to happen after a mysterious package arrives.

*A Sneak Peek at*

# Gunpowder and Tea Cakes

*My Journey with Felicity*

Meet Felicity and take a journey back in time in a book that lets *you* decide what happens.

**M**y grandmother's antiques shop is in a really old brick building in Williamsburg, Virginia. Her shop isn't crammed with all kinds of stuff like some antiques stores. Everything is tidy, and she doesn't sell anything that isn't at least a hundred years old. Some of her things are more than two hundred years old.

When I open the door, there are no customers inside. "Hi, Grandma," I call.

To my surprise, Grandma and my dad come out of the back office. Dad runs his own plumbing business, and he's hardly ever home so early.

He smiles. "Hey, how's your day been?"

Everything comes pouring out. "Dad, Lauren is picking out a new puppy this afternoon, and she invited Amara and me to go! Can I? Please? Maybe we could meet them at the animal shelter."

"I'm sorry," he says, "but I just stopped home for a minute. I have an emergency call. An elderly woman has a burst pipe and water all over her kitchen."

"You could just drop me off, and Lauren's mother will drive me home. Please?"

Dad just shakes his head. "I haven't met Lauren's

mother yet. I'm sure you'll have plenty of chances to
see the puppy."

*But I want to help choose the puppy*, I mutter in my
head. I can't have a dog because the apartment we
share with Grandma above the shop is small. We have
a sweet yellow cat named Muffy, but Grandma thinks
a dog would be too much trouble.

Dad starts to walk away, then turns back. "Cheer
up, Pumpkin."

I sigh. Dad has called me that since I was a little
kid. Today it makes me feel like he thinks I'm still a
little kid.

"We have a fun day planned for tomorrow, remember?" Dad is saying. "A daddy-daughter day at
Colonial Williamsburg."

Colonial Williamsburg is a big historic park very
close to where we live. People called interpreters work
there. They dress up in old-time costumes to tell the
story of the American Revolution, when the thirteen
colonies broke free of British rule to become the United
States of America. Sometimes they give tours of the old
buildings. Sometimes the staff and volunteers at Colonial Williamsburg stage little plays right in the streets,

and visitors can pretend they're townspeople.

My dad is a volunteer interpreter there, playing the role of a Patriot who wants independence. I've been accepted as a junior interpreter for the summer. I'll probably learn how to churn butter and bake bread, stuff like that. I agreed to do it because Dad wanted me to, but honestly, it's not how I would choose to spend my summer vacation. I'm a little worried that I won't know what to talk to visitors about. And going to Colonial Williamsburg doesn't take the place of choosing a puppy.

"Don't wait dinner on me," Dad tells Grandma. Then he walks out the door.

"It's not fair," I mumble. "He's the strictest dad on the planet. Last week I asked if I could take horseback riding lessons, and he said I had to be sixteen years old before I could."

"Your dad was afraid you might get hurt if you take riding lessons," Grandma says. "And his rule about always knowing who you're with is just to keep you safe."

As if going to an animal shelter is dangerous! "It's like he doesn't trust me. He says I'm too young to babysit, even during the day. I'm not a little kid any-more!"

Grandma shakes her head. "He's the parent. I can't second-guess his decisions."

*So*, I think, *I'm out of luck.*

Grandma changes the subject. "How was school today?"

I shrug. "School was okay. I have a lot of home-work."

"I have some homework too," she says. "I pur-chased a treasure this afternoon, and I want to learn more about it. Want to see?"

She leads me to one of the glass display cases. Inside is a teensy-tiny portrait of a woman, strung on a fine chain like a necklace. Only the woman's head and shoulders show, but it's hard to see the details. Hon-estly, I don't know why an artist would go to so much trouble.

"What good was such a little portrait?" I ask.

"This miniature was painted in 1775—right around the time of the American Revolution," Grandma says. "Imagine what life was like before photographs and videos. If people were going to be separated for some reason, these tiny portraits helped keep memories close." Grandma closes the case so the portrait won't get dusty. "Well," she says, "shall we go upstairs and cook dinner? We're having spaghetti."

"Is it okay if I don't come up for a little while?" I ask. I take a special cleaning cloth from the stack under the counter, pretending I'm going to do chores. The truth is that I really need some time by myself.

"Of course," Grandma says. "I'll call you when dinner's ready." She locks the front door, puts the "Closed" sign in the window, and goes upstairs.

At least Grandma trusts me to dust her antiques, I think. Even if Dad doesn't trust me to do anything.

I give the case holding Grandma's new miniature a swipe. Then I open the door and lean closer, studying the lady. She's very pretty. And even though her hairstyle and clothes are old-fashioned, there's something about her expression that reminds me of my mother.

My throat closes up like it does whenever I think of my mother, and I get this tight feeling inside. Suddenly I miss Mom so much it's hard to breathe.

Before Mom died, I knew I was going to miss her. Mom was the one who really encouraged me when I told my parents I want to be a veterinarian one day. She said she knew I could learn everything I need to learn if I set my mind to it.

Dad hardly ever mentions Mom, so I don't either. But everything would be different if she were still alive. I never felt as if I were being treated like a baby when Mom was around.

Gently, very gently, I pick up the tiny painting. The woman in the miniature portrait looks kind and understanding. It seems as if she's staring right into my eyes.

But something's wrong. The painted colors blur. I start to feel dizzy, so I squinch my eyes closed. The floor tilts beneath my feet. Everything whirls around. I know I mustn't drop the miniature, so I clench it in my hand. I'm really confused—and scared, too. What is going on?

Before I can open my eyes, I hear shouting. It comes from a distance at first, but grows louder. The whirling feeling fades. The noise keeps getting louder, though. I open my eyes . . . and I have to fight away dizziness again, because I am not in my grandma's antiques shop!

Somehow I ended up outside, huddled behind a thick green hedge. All the commotion is coming from the other side of the hedge. Feet pound as if somebody is running. Men and women are yelling, and . . . is that hoofbeats? I have to see what's happening!

I spot an opening in the hedge, but when I start to hurry through, I trip and fall. I land hard on a walkway of crushed oyster shells. "Ow!"

"Have a care!" someone says. "'Tis a poor day to stumble, in this crowd."

It's a girl about my own age. Instead of shorts or jeans, she's wearing a long purple-striped gown—the kind of dress interpreters wear at Colonial Williamsburg.

"Are you a volunteer?" I blurt.

"That fall must have addled you," the girl says. "Only boys may volunteer."

She gives me a hand up, and I stagger to my feet. I finally get a good look around . . . and can hardly believe my eyes.

Am I dreaming? I wonder. Did I sleepwalk? I've never walked in my sleep before. But somehow I've ended up in Colonial Williamsburg. The big, beautiful brick building up ahead is the Governor's Palace. My dad has brought me here many times, but it's a very long walk from our house.

Interpreters are all around me, mostly hurrying in the same direction. And when I glance down, I discover I'm wearing the same kind of long dress the girl is wearing. Mine is cream-colored with little blue flowers. It's pretty, but it feels too tight. A white kerchief is tucked around my neck.

"Are you hurt?" the girl asks kindly. "My name is Felicity Merriman. What's yours?"

I tell her my name. "I—I don't think I'm hurt. But I'm confused! What is happening?"

"Have you just arrived in the city?" Felicity asks.

She must be one of the junior interpreters. She's really good, just like an actor. I decide to play along so I can sort out this mess. "It seems so."

Felicity doesn't look at all surprised. "Many have arrived since the royal governor schemed to steal the colonists' gunpowder from the Magazine in the dark of night."

My dad has explained that in colonial times, a Magazine was a place where people stored gunpowder, bullets, and other ammunition and weapons.

"Riders immediately carried the news all over the countryside," Felicity continues. "Patriots have been streaming into Williamsburg like a river in flood!"

I must be in the middle of a special event, I think. This one is really authentic. Men and women are gathering on the huge green lawn in front of the Governor's Palace. Some look curious, as if they don't know what's going on either. Some look really angry. The angry ones shout things like "Return our powder!" and "Storm the palace!"

Two barefoot little boys wearing ragged clothes run past. They're no more than five or six, but I don't see any adult keeping an eye on them. A man waves a knife that looks really sharp. A woman limps by, and I can see she has a bad scrape on one ankle. A carriage passes, jolting badly because of deep ruts in the dirt road.

But . . . that can't be. Dad and I have walked this road. It's paved.

My mouth goes dry. Something is truly and terribly wrong. It's not just that I somehow ended up in Colonial Williamsburg wearing a costume—it's that there are no modern visitors anywhere. Everything and everyone looks and sounds and feels real.

Too real. I've got to get out of here!

But how?

This all started when I picked up the miniature portrait of the pretty woman. I'd forgotten all about it, but I'm still clutching it in my left hand. I dart back through the gap in the hedge. Slowly I uncurl my fingers and stare into the painted eyes.

# About the Author

VALERIE TRIPP says that she became a writer because of the kind of person she is. She says she's curious, and writing requires you to be interested in everything. Talking is her favorite sport, and writing is a way of talking on paper. She's a daydreamer, which helps her come up with her ideas. And she loves words. She even loves the struggle to come up with just the right words as she writes and rewrites. Ms. Tripp lives in Maryland with her husband.